PLAIN JANE
THE AWAKENING

Book One of the Soul Lineage Trilogy

JACLYN BALES

Plain Jane: The Awakening
Book One of the Soul Lineage Trilogy

© 2025 Jaclyn Bales
All rights reserved.

Cover design by Keisha Reene
Editing by Megan Records
Final Proofread Ashley Emma
Interior Formatting HMD Publishing

Character and artistic imagery © Keisha Renee. Remaining chapter heading images sourced from Shutterstock or photographed by the author in New Orleans.

ISBN: [979-8-218-79341-8 paperback]
ISBN: [979-8-218-79340-1 hardcover]

First Edition: October 2025
Printed in the United States of America

CONTENTS

For those who have ever felt misunderstood. For the ones who were
misdiagnosed, mislabeled, dismissed, or ignored. For the children
who grew up too fast. For the women who were told they were "too
sensitive," "too dramatic," "too much." For anyone who has carried a
storm inside them and had to smile through the thunder. For those
who see the world in kaleidoscope colors but were told to stick to
black and white. For those who had to shrink themselves to fit. For
those who burned with magic no one else could see. This is for you. I
hear you. I see you. I feel you. You are not broken. You are not alone.
You are worthy of every happiness. And you are so much more than
they ever let you believe.

Acknowledgements

This story wouldn't exist without the voices who reminded me I wasn't alone, including my loving and supportive family.

To the women who feel they are too much, to the ones who were told they were too loud, too emotional, too different: you are the reason this book breathes. To my family and chosen family: thank you for your patience, your late-night encouragement, and your belief in this magic long before it was real. To my Digital Artist, editors, beta readers, and creative friends: thank you for seeing this story clearly and helping me shape it into something worthy of its characters. To the city of New Orleans, whose bones echo with magic: you gave Jane her heartbeat. To my daughter: you made me believe in magic again. Your wonder, your laughter, and the way you see the world remind me every day that the most powerful stories start with love.

And to every reader holding this book in their hands: thank you. You are part of the spell now.

CHAPTER ONE

THE MOON REMEMBERS

I think maybe I'm the moon after all, not the sun. Still a source of light, but one born in darkness, holding hands with every star as they flicker through the night. I light quiet paths through fog and forest, changing shape beneath watchful eyes, falling and rising again and again.

I wake to my breath catching. Another dream. Another version of me I can almost remember. Always close. Never clear. The same ache presses behind my ribs, a soft pull, like gravity or grief, begging me to remember something I've never been told. The air smells like rain and lavender and something…older. A chill curls down my spine. Not from fear—from recognition. Like something is coming. Or maybe returning.

Moonlight spills across the ceiling, painting soft silver over the cracked plaster. I hadn't meant to fall asleep—not really. But I didn't sleep well last night, and tonight is the book club. We meet every month under the crescent moon in Jackson Square—a midnight gathering by candlelight where we read, drink tea, and try not to notice how the air always seems to shift when the clock strikes twelve.

I'd set an alarm, swearing I'd only nap for an hour. But judging by the shadows stretching across the floor, I must've slept deeper than I intended.

I sit up, wiping the sweat from my brow, and wonder absently if I was talking in my sleep again. The apartments above our magic shop are cloaked for privacy, but I still sometimes worry my grandmother might hear something. She never says anything, but she knows things. She always knows.

I drag myself out of bed and into the bathroom, flicking on the light and turning the tap toward hot. Lavender oil. A few drops of vetiver. Anything to wash this weight off my chest.

Steam curls against the mirror as I step into the shower, letting it scald the restlessness away. But the moment I close my eyes, it returns—the face. That stranger. Still not clear. Still shrouded in dreamlight. But closer.

This time, when I see him—his form just behind the veil of sleep—I feel a flicker beneath my skin. Like static. A prickling at the base of my neck. Heat pulses through my hands and spreads across my collarbone. The steam thickens strangely, and when I open my eyes, the mirror is completely fogged except for one small space. A symbol. A faint crescent shape etched in condensation. I blink, and it's gone.

But I felt it. The shift. The presence.

I press my palms to the tile, heart thudding now, because something's changed. For the first time, I heard his name.

Alexander.

I whispered it—said it like I'd always known it—and just before he spoke mine in return, I woke. We were embracing, like lovers, like the end of something that had never properly begun.

And the second I whisper it, I swear I feel his breath at my neck.

My stomach flips. My breath stutters.

His name. I finally know his name.

The man in the shadows. The one in every dream. The presence I think I've felt watching me for the past couple of years. The ache I could never explain.

Two weeks until my thirtieth birthday. Just fourteen days until the blood moon rises again. And whatever I am—whoever I was—is beginning to wake up.

The shower warms around me, but my thoughts stay sharp. Sharper than they've been in weeks. I've always known I was a witch—born into the magic like every woman in our family before me. But what I carry has never bloomed fully. Not like it did in Gran. Not like the stories in our grimoire.

It flickers like low embers under ash. Psychic energy, little visions. Healing touch. Enough to give ghost tours, read cards, help Gran with tinctures and salves for love or grief or sleeplessness. But the deeper power? The legacy? It hides. Or waits.

Gran says it's because I was born under strange skies. The moon rose blood-red—a harvest moon, swollen and rare. People said the sky bled that night, and the world held its breath. Gran has always said that it wasn't just a coincidence, especially since the rare celestial event is coming back around for my birthday.

I step out, wrap a towel around myself, and glance at the clock. Shit. It's later than I thought.

My anxiety kicks into high gear, but thankfully, so does my over-preparation. My tote is already mostly packed—everything except the tea. I throw on jeans and a vintage tee, the cotton soft and familiar against my skin. I left a sweater in my bag just in case the breeze picks up. I double-check. Triple check. Still feel like I'm forgetting something.

Socks. Sneakers. My hair still damp and wild, but that's nothing new. I run a comb through it once and call it good. My key pendant never comes off, not even in the shower. It's the only jewelry I typically wear unless I'm going out for something special; even then, it's with me always. A gift from my Gran for my 16th birthday. It helps channel what little power I have, but she said she also spelled it with grounding magic as well to help with my anxiety. She is the best like that.

I swipe on a little blush and a dab of lip stain—nothing more. I've never been much of a makeup girl. Give me jeans, a T-shirt, and some candlelight, and I'm good. Besides, I've gotten a little sun lately. My skin's glowing on its own.

Fully dressed, I sling my bag over my shoulder and head downstairs through the shop. There's a private back exit to my apartment, but I want to see Gran before I leave.

The Séance & Sundry smells of clove, chamomile, and the faint trace of patchouli. Candles flicker on the high shelf where we keep the dried herbs, even though no one's touched them. A bundle of yarrow glows faintly under the window where the moonlight spills in. The wards hum a little louder than usual, like the shop itself is stirring with me.

As I pass the register, it lets out a soft click—phantom habit, or maybe just the shop's way of saying hello. From the back office, I hear Gran muttering about ledger numbers.

There's a framed photo in the corner behind the display case. My mother, young and smiling, arm around Gran in front of the original storefront. I never met her, but I know her eyes. They're mine.

I grab my tea thermoses—one for me, one for Braelynn, who I know will forgot to bring anything to drink. I toss in an extra blanket too, and a candle lantern for reading. She's my best friend, but the woman is chronically unprepared.

I chuckle to myself as I pop the thermoses in my bag. She'll bring the book. Hopefully.

This is where my anxiety and ADHD dance in circles—my brain forgets, but also won't let me forget. I check everything again. Yes, candles—but did I pack matches?

Nope.

I slide open the drawer by the register, grab a box, and toss it in.

The vintage bell above the door jingles as I step out into the night.

"I love you!" I call out behind me. "Book club's meeting for the midnight moonlight read. See you in the morning!"

Gran's voice floats back, warm as ever: "Bye, Janey! Be safe and have fun. No late-night cemetery walks on your way back—you hear me? Lock up behind you. Love you!"

That nickname always gets me. Janey.

She's been my whole world since I was born.

My mom and dad died the night I came into this world, but Gran... she stepped in like she was always meant to. She's more than a grandmother. More than a mother. She's a compass. A fire. The soft place I land when the world is too loud.

She used to brush my hair every night as a kid, even when I was too old for it. Just to calm me down. Just to say, "You don't have to explain, baby. I already know."

And somehow, she always does. Like she knew I planned to stop by the cemetery later. How does she know?

Because she's a witch. Because she knows everything.

But more than her knowing—she loves me in all of it. In the mess. In the magic. In the tangle of my mind.

She gives the best hugs. The kind you feel in your bones.

I smile as I walk into the warm, humming darkness of the Quarter, tote in hand, the moon just beginning to glow. The crescent moon hangs like a curved blade in the sky, cutting just enough light through the dark to make shadows simmer.

The Quarter pulses with quiet magic—iron-laced balconies dripping with ferns, gaslamps flickering like fireflies in mourning. The cobblestones beneath my sneakers still hold the day's heat. Music drifts in from somewhere—lazy jazz or something older, woven into the bones of the city. The air is thick with praline sugar, river salt, and whispered secrets. Even the shadows here seemed to hum.

As I round the corner, I pause just briefly. A dog howls somewhere in the distance. Someone brushes past me, too close, too slow, his eyes locked on mine for a breath longer than polite. His hair in a white blonde mohawk, so bright it almost appeared to glow. My pulse stutters. But when I glance back, he's gone.

Tonight is The Crescent City book club. And something inside me feels like it's waiting for more than just a story.

WHY
PHISPY

WHERE THE MOON
MEETS THE STONE

I'm late.

Not late-late, but late enough to send my mood into that tight coil of anxiety that lives just below my collarbone. And now I'll be sweaty, out of breath, and overthinking everything I say for the rest of the night. Classic Jane. I glance at the time again, even though it hasn't changed since the last five times I checked it. Just in case the universe wants to grant me a miracle.

It's not even my fault. The nap was necessary. Essential, really. But still, the members of the Crescent Read don't exactly wait around for anyone. Not even for me.

The streets hum beneath my Converse as I cut through the Quarter, shoulders slightly hunched, arms clutching my tote like it holds the last of my dignity. The French Quarter at night is never quiet, even off-season. It breathes like something alive—music echoing from a courtyard three blocks away, laughter slipping out from open bar doors, a saxophone trailing along the wind like perfume.

The scent of fried shrimp and powdered sugar dances with the damp river breeze. This part of the city always feels like a story already in progress—every flickering gaslamp and weathered step holds a secret.

The moon is bright overhead, despite being in its sharp crescent form, swaddled in mist and brilliance. Its light spills over the cobblestones and ironwork balconies, silvering the city in a way that always feels like a secret. It's the kind of night that makes you believe in ghosts. Or love. Or both.

My knockoff earbuds hum against the edges of my ears. I don't like the kind that go inside—they make my ears sore, like they're intruding. These I found on TikTok just rest gently over the top. Not glamorous, but effective.

Stevie Nicks's voice begins to float in, ironically, her song New Orleans. And just like that, my mood softens.

A smile tugs at the corner of my lips as I remember that day three years ago, when I was leaning over my balcony with a hot cup of chicory coffee in hand, only to see her. Stevie. Standing across the way on a terrace near the Royal Orleans Hotel. A soft scarf in her hand, wind in her silver-blonde hair. We made eye contact. She gave me the smallest nod. A knowing smile.

Her eyes met mine like she saw something in me—something old. I remember standing there frozen, coffee cooling in my hands, wondering if she knew something I didn't.

I'm not saying it was magic. But I'm also not saying it wasn't.

I've always believed Stevie was extraordinary—not a witch exactly, just something else. Something empathetic and healing and electric. Her voice settles into the bones like a tonic. And tonight, it helps me breathe.

I glance up at the cathedral in the distance—our sacred meeting spot. The Crescent Read has gathered there every crescent moon for nearly two years now. Always at midnight, for no other reason than that's what we chose. Always with a shared book and candlelight. NOLA's coven and pack joining together for something simple. It was a small group, but it was a cute tradition.

We started Crescent Read after a wine-fueled debate about soulmates in fantasy books turned into a midnight walk through the Quarter. By the next crescent moon, we had candles, a reading list, and a sacred spot under the cathedral.

Tonight's pick? *Haunting Adeline* by H.D. Carlton.

Dark fantasy, shadow obsession, psychological spice. I'd pretend to be shocked at Braelynn for picking it for the book club, but I know better.

I won't lie—not out loud, at least—this one's got its hooks in me. There's something about the idea of being watched, studied, craved. It shouldn't appeal to me, but…

It does.

Maybe it's because I've felt watched for years now. Just out of sight. Around corners. In mirrors. In dreams. In every shadow.

Maybe it's just in my head.

Or maybe…it isn't.

Just as Stevie hits the chorus, I feel the hairs on my neck rise—too late.

"Jesus Christ!" I practically scream, leaping back a foot like a cartoon character mid-exorcism. My heart does a somersault in my chest as I whip around to find the grinning face of my best friend, book in hand…and absolutely nothing else.

No blanket. No tea. No light source—not even a candle or a lantern.

"Seriously, B?" I exhale, hand still clutching my chest like I'm eighty and just lost a round of bingo. "Why do you do that? You know I zone out."

She shrugs with the smuggest look known to womankind. "You're welcome. Call it cardio."

Brealynn—my bestie. Curvy, striking looks, caramel-toned skin that glows under the moonlight, her natural black curls pinned back just enough to frame her face. Dressed in her usual leather jacket and bold hoop earrings. She always looks like she's on her way to punch a vampire or kiss one—or maybe both.

We're different in every possible way, yet somehow the exact same where it matters.

People don't talk about platonic soulmates enough. They should.

I met B sophomore year, after I switched schools through school of choice. I didn't fit anywhere, not really, until she sat beside me in homeroom. It wasn't dramatic—just a smile, a joke about the teacher, and then suddenly I wasn't alone anymore. From that moment on, it was like something in the universe clicked into place. We've always said we're platonic soulmates, and I believe it. She's my chosen family, the piece of me I didn't know was missing until she arrived.

She's my sister from another mister, the one human being I can't hide from. Not with words, not with sarcasm, not with spiritual bypassing or tea.

B has this uncanny talent for crashing into my life exactly when I'm spiraling. Once I was crying over some jerk who broke up with me by text, and she showed up at my door with a pint of ice cream and a pack of tarot cards. She took one look at me and said, "Don't worry, the cards already told me he has erectile dysfunction in his future." I laughed so hard I forgot why I was upset. That's B—equal parts comfort and chaos, always ready to roast my pain into oblivion until it doesn't hurt anymore.

She sees me. Because of her, I've faced things about myself I used to bury under politeness and people-pleasing. She's the reason I stopped apologizing for taking up space and started learning how to be. Neurodivergence, anxiety, magical quirks and all.

She's taught me that I don't have to earn love by shrinking. I'm allowed to just be loved.

Braelynn squints at me, all smug. "Damn, J. You're so salty, I'm getting flashbacks to Margarita Monday."

I snort without looking up. "Please, bitch. You cried over a tortilla chip and blamed the moon for your emotional outburst!"

We dissolve into laughter, the kind that includes full-body wheezing and teary-eyed gasps. The kind that draws stares from passersby and makes the Quarter feel like ours for a moment.

Which is fitting, considering we're just a few steps away from Jackson Square, and the Crescent Read is waiting.

I glance over at B and ask, "Hey, you're still coming over tomorrow, right? To help me rearrange the shop and set out a few things for the upcoming full moon special?"

She looks at me and groans. "Shit. I think I was gonna shift tomorrow. The moon's been climbing and I haven't had a decent run all month."

She means her wolf shift, of course. I kind of figured, since she wasn't planning to shift tonight. Because she comes from one of the older bloodlines of wolves, she has the ability to shift outside of the full moon. Older bloodlines tend to run packs because they have more power and control over their abilities. For a majority of the wolves, though, they have to shift at least once in the 3-day window of the full moon. Typically, they don't have a choice the first few shifts, and it happens during the peak day around puberty. After those first few shifts, they get more control—but they still have to shift at least once during that window. I smile, "Pretty sure it's not even full yet." B just grins back sarcastically, "You know it doesn't have to be, I always do better on build-up nights anyways. More edge, but less chaos."

I laugh. "Isn't moon chaos kind of like your brand?"

She gives me a big, mischievous smile. "I can definitely save it for a later day if Gran's planning on making gumbo."

I laugh. "How did you not remember this? I literally texted it to you! All you had to do was click the link—it adds right to your iPhone calendar."

She lets out a full, hearty laugh, looking at me like I've grown a second head. "Girl, I don't know nothin' about an iPhone calendar. I don't do that."

I stare at her, laughing but genuinely shocked. "What do you mean? You can set reminders, color-code it, everything. Don't tell me you still use that busted day planner and write everything down when you've got a whole-ass calendar in your pocket."

She laughs even harder. "Why do I need reminders? I have you for that."

I roll my eyes. "I don't know why I'm surprised, considering you've got like a bazillion notifications on your phone. That would drive me cuckoo bananas—not to clear those out? And don't even get me started on that email you can't get into."

She grins. "Okay, Grandma. Who even says cuckoo bananas any-more?"

I side-eye her with a smirk and a small chuckle. "Yeah, okay. Says the girl who literally just admitted she still uses a day planner."

I swear, I can't get enough of our talks. It doesn't matter how often we see each other or how many years go by—we always find something to laugh about.

I shift my weight on the blanket, flipping the page with one hand and sipping tea with the other.

"Wait…" I murmur, peeking toward the cathedral's iron gate. "Where's Maurice? He's usually here first, spreading out enough snacks to feed a small army."

Brealynn snorts. "Probably stopped to flirt with someone or rescue a lost dog."

"So he's probably not coming tonight?"

Even before I see him, I catch the hint of his cologne—cedar and bourbon and something wolfish beneath. Heavy footsteps crunch over loose stone, a low grunt cutting through the quiet. My pulse lifts, even before he emerges from the mist like some too-handsome local legend carrying snacks and judgment.

As if summoned by name—or possibly by sheer sass—Maurice stumbles through the haze, tripping slightly over the uneven cobble-stones with a dramatic "whoa" and a half-spilled bag of supplies under one arm.

"And here I was thinking y'all might miss me," he says with a crook-ed grin, recovering quickly and flashing dimples like weapons. He glances between us with warm eyes that crinkle at the corners. "But I see my cousin's already replaced me with tea and the drama."

"You're late," I say, trying not to laugh.

"I brought snacks, a pillow, and emotional support," he says, plop-ping down beside us and pulling a fleece blanket over his lap with the kind of efficiency that says: yes, this man reads under the moon regularly. "And a citronella candle. You're welcome."

Braelynn elbows him. "Why are you like this?" Maurice grins. "Built different. Born to annoy." We all laugh—loud, loose, familiar. There's an ease when Maurice is around. A kind of quiet joy that wraps around you like soft denim.

He's…always been like that.

Maurice, Braelynn's cousin through his dad's marriage to her aunt. My friend.

Six-foot-six-inches of Creole charm and werewolf energy, with strong arms, gentle hands, and that thick, dark curl of hair—now shaped into a tight bald fade that leads up to a crown of coiled curls. Rugged in a way that doesn't demand attention but earns it naturally.

His voice is low and warm, like honey poured over a record scratch.

And that smile…God, that smile.

He's always been B's big cousin and my accidental protector. The one who walks us home without asking. The one who notices when your voice wavers, even if you're laughing. The one who shows up.

Maurice has this habit of turning into my bodyguard without meaning to. Sophomore year, a guy twice my size cut in front of me in the lunch line, and before I could even open my mouth, Maurice stepped between us like it was instinct. He didn't growl or throw a punch—he just gave the guy a look. You know the kind. The guy backed off, muttering about how it wasn't worth it. Maurice shrugged and went back to debating comic books with me like nothing had happened. That's the thing about him—he doesn't even realize he does it. He just protects me, like it's muscle memory.

And yeah—there's always been something there. A pull. A heat. A "what if" I keep tucked away behind my ribs.

There was one night a few years ago…late and stupid and hot. A party. Too much rum. We danced too close, touched too long. We kissed like we'd done it a thousand times before, and when we went upstairs into a room, hands wandered. Shirts came off. We got as far as the edge of no return before—

I stopped.

My anxiety clenched like a fist in my chest. My voice cracked on the word wait.

I remember the heat of his palm against the small of my back, the way his lips brushed mine like they already belonged there. But something in me froze—too fast, too full, like standing at the edge of a cliff you've dreamed about but never thought you'd reach. My heart was racing. My mind was loud. And he just held me like that was enough.

No questions. No pressure. Just kindness in his eyes as he pulled the blanket around us instead.

We never talked about it again.

But sometimes, I still think about how he was the closest I've ever come to letting someone in.

And yet, every time I reach for more, something inside me recoils.

Is it because my soul belongs to someone else? Even if I don't know who. Even if I haven't met him in this life yet. Is it because I fear complicating something that is already perfect and ruining the dynamics of not only our friendship, but the group's, mostly with B? Is it both? I couldn't say.

Maurice catches me staring.

"You alright, Jane Agatha?" he asks softly.

"You're the only one who uses my full name."

"Gotta keep you humble," he says.

"BJ forever!" B chimes in, throwing her arm around me.

"See?!" Maurice groans. "I'll never be okay with being left out."

"You're not in the B and J club," I tease.

"Neither are Fergus or Javi!" he argues.

"Exactly," B smirks. "This is girl core, babe."

We all crack up, laughter echoing into the warm night. There was something about our group—even missing our other two besties—that always felt right. Whole. B and Maurice were found family, more than just friends for me.

Fergus, our cinnamon-haired, freckled Irish werewolf, migrated to our New Orleans Crescent City Pack from the Ironwood Grove Pack, was probably somewhere tossing back a pint and howling at the moon, shirt half open, freckles glowing in bar light.

And Javi, our tall, glam-as-hell drag witch—sorcerer as he calls himself—was off enchanting mortals and slaying runway shows on tour until next week, likely wearing six-inch heels and conjuring cocktails with a snap of his fingers. He could turn the air into glitter with a wink and a hair flip.

We're an eclectic little crew.

B, daughter of the current pack master, carries a legacy no woman has ever held before. If she steps into leadership, she'd be the first. And while she shrugs it off in public, I know it weighs on her.

The first time I saw her shift, I was stunned.

Her wolf form was all white—unheard of in the New Orleans pack—with a single black streak down her shoulders and back. Her green eyes glow, kissed with gold at the edges. Majestic. Powerful. Rare.

And Maurice? He'd burn the world down to protect her.

If it ever came to it, he'd lead in her place—but only to shield her from the cost. That's who he is.

And me?

One day, I'll lead the NOLA coven. Like Gran. Like my bloodline before me.

Two women. Two legacies. Moon and magic.

I lean back, watching them bicker as the moon rises over the cathedral.

Then it hits me again. That feeling again of being watched. Not by a stranger. Not like a creep in the shadows. No. This feels…known. Ancient. Familiar. My spine tingles like static. The air thickens—not heavy, not sharp. Just charged.

Like I've brushed up against a memory that doesn't belong to me.

My stomach flips. My breath stills. And somewhere inside, a voice I've never heard whispers: He's near.

TANGLED ROOTS

The feeling of being watched faded as quickly as it came.

By the time I blinked myself back into the present, the quiet had shifted. Maurice and B were no longer teasing each other—both had settled into their respective books, brows furrowed and pages turning in rhythm. The muggy New Orleans night wrapped around them like a second skin, thick with the scent of magnolia and sweet spice from the nearby street vendors.

I tried to read too, but my thoughts kept slipping. My fingers brushed the page, but my mind clung to the name I wasn't supposed to know. Alexander. A name from a dream, and yet somehow real.

About an hour passed before I finally closed my book with a quiet sigh.

"I'm gonna call it for tonight," I said, stretching out my legs on the stone bench.

Maurice didn't even look up. "Good. I was getting sick of glancing over and seeing Braelynn licking her lips at her book like it was a damn beignet," he said, side-eyeing us both with a smirk. "And you? Blushing like a Southern bride on her honeymoon. Had me wondering what the hell y'all were reading."

B grinned wickedly. "You should get this book. Might teach you a thing or two."

I chuckled, heat rising to my cheeks as Maurice tossed me a sly glance. I could read exactly what was behind those eyes—and it had nothing to do with plotlines or paperbacks. He mostly chooses his own book, which we've tried to explain isn't how a book club works, but he insists. He has read maybe 3 or 4 of the same books with us over the years.

B stood and stretched. "I'm good to wrap up early anyway," she said, rolling her shoulders. "My wolf energy's been buzzing all day. This upcoming Blood Moon energy has got me twitchy. Since I'm saving my shift for later, I might just blow off some steam with a sexy tourist tonight."

I smirked. "Classy."

Maurice laughed. "You would."

I nudged him. "Like both of us haven't done the same. Only mine's usually boredom-driven."

Maurice waggled his eyebrows. "Want me to help with that?"

"Nope," I said quickly, laughing and turning my face away. "Are you gonna do the same?"

He shook his head. "Nah. I'll shift tonight. Go for a run. Got too much pent-up energy and a lot on my mind. But first, I'm walking Braelynn to wherever the hell she's partying—and then I'm walking you home."

I narrowed my eyes. "No, you're not. I'm going for a walk myself. You try to play guard dog, I'll zap you."

Maurice held up his hands. "Oh hell no. Not the zap."

"I didn't mean to last time," I said innocently. "You know I can't always control how strong it is during the full moon. Just meant to tickle your side. Little static shock."

"Little?!" he scoffed. "Felt like you tasered my spleen."

We all laughed, stuffing books into bags and slinging them over our shoulders. Jackson Square had mostly emptied, leaving behind the hum of street lamps and faint jazz drifting from Bourbon Street. Maurice, being B's cousin on her mom's side, is also part of her old bloodline with the ability to control his shift.

B looked at us both, grinning. "Y'all are too much. You should just fuck and get it over with already."

If only she knew how close we had come before I thought to myself. I barked a laugh. "Pass."

Maurice slung an arm over each of our shoulders. "Yeah, 'cause if we did, she'd fall head over heels in love with me. Then our friendship would be ruined. And I'm emotionally unavailable, obviously."

B doubled over laughing. "Keep dreaming, Wolf Boy."

Maurice talks a big game about being emotionally unavailable, but the truth is, he feels everything too deeply. I've never once seen him with anyone—just a trail of jokes and walls he pretends are thicker than they really are.

As we turned toward Bourbon, I gave B a mischievous glance. "So… what kind of tourist are you hunting tonight?"

"Whoever sparks the mood, I guess," she said with a wink. "But I think I'm gonna go for a girl again. At least with them, I never have to fake it."

Maurice groaned. "Too much info for your cousin."

I snorted. "No, I think I know what you mean."

B raised a finger like she was making a TED Talk. "Look. Eighty percent of women can't orgasm without clitoral stimulation. Eighty percent. And somehow these dudes think every woman is just magically coming from their dicks alone. Like, no, sir. It's not an on-off switch. It's a symphony, and y'all keep bringing a damn kazoo."

I nearly choked. "Okay, okay! You're not wrong. I mean, you both know I don't have extensive experience or anything, but with what experience I do have…I gotta agree with you. A lot of them really don't know what they're doing."

They began to banter, giving me space—and that's all it took for the spiral of thoughts to start.

I can count the number of people I've had intimate experiences with on two hands. I've just never been one of those people who could have a one-night stand or kiss a random stranger. There's nothing wrong with that—hell, I sometimes wish I could be that free. But for me, intimacy has always felt…vulnerable. Like something that required safety, trust, and some kind of connection before I could even think about opening up in that way.

There was this one tourist. We met on a ghost tour—he was in town for work. First time in New Orleans. He came back a few times over six months, and we kept hanging out. I started to think it might become something more…but then his position changed, and the calls just stopped. I tried not to take it personally, but I was disappointed.

Sometimes there were others—tourists who were here for a weekend. If we vibed, I'd hang out, get to know them, and if it felt right, maybe it'd go further…but never on the first night. Never just for the sake of it, even though I crack jokes about boredom-driven hookups.

The first time I had sex, I was fourteen. I didn't even know what it was supposed to feel like or what an orgasm was. He was the first boy who ever paid me attention. I gave in because I thought that was what I was supposed to do. I'd been bullied so badly in high school. The girls used to yell "Plain Jane" every time I walked by, laughing like it was some brilliant insult. They were all into makeup tutorials and trendy brands. I am curvy, always a jeans-and-T-shirt kind of girl, always looking a little undone. Still kinda do.

Even the younger girls in the coven had their ways of teasing me. They got their powers early, magic buzzing just under their skin once puberty hit, while I had very little of anything. "Leave it to Plain Jane, nothing special in any way, even the way she is meant to be special."

And then there was the only serious relationship I ever had. Almost two years. He was great—smart, kind. But when he got his degree, he wanted to leave New Orleans. I couldn't go with him. This city is home. My roots are already deep here. I love the idea of travel, sure, but this is where I want to build something that lasts.

I blinked and looked up, suddenly aware of how long I'd been quiet. Braelynn and Maurice were watching me, both with soft smiles.

"I'm sorry," I said, regretting the words instantly.

B shook her head, voice gentle. "Girl, you don't have to apologize. I love you just how you are. Take whatever time you need in thought—and never apologize for taking up space or being you."

That lump rose in my throat again. I smiled, eyes burning as I blinked fast. They've always made me feel so safe. So seen. When we met as teens, B was the one who always snapped me out of my imposter syndrome. By my mid-twenties, I'd found my confidence—but some days, the cracks still showed.

B has such a big heart, and I know she has a thing for someone lately. A particular wolf from a neighboring splinter pack who has recently started joining city patrols. Her name is Kaia Ruelle—she's a few years younger, but sharp and unbothered in that cocky, cool-girl way. Olive-toned skin, chestnut-brown eyes, and a choppy platinum bob with black roots. Kaia worked as a tattoo artist, and rumor had it her ink carried glyphs of protection, memory, and vows too sacred to speak aloud. She'd split from her pack after a fight with her alpha over gender roles, and since then, she's been living quietly in New Orleans. Tough, independent, and magnetic—exactly the kind of girl Braelynn would fall for, and exactly the kind that might run if things got too real.

B never talked about it. But I could tell.

After a beat, I shifted the subject. "Have you heard from Javi?"

Maurice's face softened. "Not since he left on his tour. But you two usually talk about that stuff more—it's kinda girl talk."

B and I shared a knowing laugh.

"I haven't heard either," I said. "I don't think he stopped by his parents' house like he said he might. Or if he did, it didn't go well."

B's jaw clenched. "I hope he's okay. I mean, Fergus was able to patch things up a bit with his folks, but Javi's parents are another level of douchebag. If they hurt him, I swear I'll go kick their asses myself."

Javi De la Rosa had been raised in a deeply religious Latin household—one that viewed witchcraft as sin even though they were witches themselves, and queerness as worse. When he came out as gay and refused to hide his magic or his love of performing in drag, they cut him off. He hadn't looked back since. The coven took him in, and New Orleans became his new home, but some scars ran deeper than any spell could fix. I had hoped this trip would offer closure. But knowing Javi, he probably got as far as the street before turning away.

I nodded slowly. I would join Bree on that trip, no question.

As for Fergus, his story carried a different edge. He'd come over from Ireland years ago, worn down by the traditional expectations of his old pack—especially the arranged marriage set for him since birth. It didn't matter if you found a true wolf mate, something no one could control; his pack cared more about unions that were advantageous. Leaving it all behind, Fergus carved out a new life in New Orleans, eventually opening a bar in the Quarter. Rough around the edges but soft at his core, he'd only recently begun trying to mend things with his family. His parents had visited a few months back, and while it wasn't perfect, it was a start. I hoped Javi could have something like that one day too.

As we neared the main hub of the Quarter, the sounds of live music, laughter, and drunken joy buzzed louder. It was time to split.

I hugged B first. "Be safe. Love you."

"You too. Love you," B called, already wandering off toward the Carousel Bar, hips swaying with confident ease.

I turned to Maurice. "Have a good run."

He hesitated. "You going straight home? Or one of your moonlit cemetery strolls?"

I gave him a soft look. "Don't worry. I'm a big girl. I might not have all my powers, but I've got enough. And I know how to fight. You taught me."

It was true. After I'd been robbed a few years back, Maurice had trained me himself. Now I could hold my own—and I had a nasty electric zap in my arsenal tonight. Leading up to the Blood Moon, it seems things are sparking a little more than usual.

Maurice grinned. "You can handle yourself. But I still don't like it."

I smirked. "I'm a witch in New Orleans. It's practically my civic duty to walk in a cemetery under the light of the moon!"

He laughed then—deeply from his belly. It warmed my chest more than I wanted to admit.

I cleared my throat. "You gonna stop by Fergus's bar?"

"Probably not. Tourist crowds are wild. He'll be slammed. I'll swing by tomorrow if he's not on patrol."

Then he grabbed me in a bear hug, lifted me off the ground, and spun me around. "Hope your walk gives you what you need. Be safe, witch."

"You too, Wolf Boy."

And with that, we parted ways.

My footsteps echoed against the stone as I headed toward St. Louis Cemetery No. 1. The night air was thick with moonlight and secrets. I thought maybe I'd stop by Marie Laveau's grave tonight.

Just to pay my respects.

Or maybe to ask a few questions.

CHAPTER FOUR

GRAVE INTENTIONS

The streets grow quieter the farther I walk, the last echo of jazz dissolving behind me like a memory.

I know this path by heart—each cracked sidewalk, each flickering gas lamp, each mural half-hidden behind ironwork and vines. New Orleans doesn't sleep, not really. But she does quiet at night, pulling her magic in close, like a shawl against the shoulders of her people.

And this—this cemetery—is her heart.

St. Louis No. 1 is where the veils feel thinnest. It's where the old bones rest in rows of white stone and crumbling offerings, where whispers move like wind between tombs and history breathes beneath your feet.

I love it here. Always have.

Not in the way tourists love it—with hushed reverence or performative fear—but in the way you love a home you never had to earn.

This place knows me.

Here, I'm not too much or too strange. Here, I don't need to explain why I feel everything thanks to extreme empathy. The locals don't just tolerate the supernatural—they live beside it. Balance is understood. The two-natured—witches, wolves, seers—don't hide in shadows. They guide, protect, heal.

Tourists come for the jazz, the food, and the ghost stories, but they only ever see the surface. The two-natured move quietly beneath it all, stitched into the city's rhythm like a second heartbeat. Locals don't fear them; they dance to the same song, an old balance New Orleans has always kept.

Even those without magic glow with something else entirely: resilience. Joy. Spirit. That strange, intangible electricity that hums through second lines and storm-prep prayers. A different kind of magic. One that doesn't need spells or bloodlines.

And in this city—my city—it's enough.

I reach the gates of the cemetery.

They're tall, wrought-iron, and chained shut for the night. Past a certain hour—after the last ghost tour stumbles off with their plastic wine cups and staged screams—the gates are locked to the rest of the world.

But not to me.

I slide my hand into my T-shirt, fingers wrapping around the smooth back of my pendant. It's shaped like a key for a reason.

I close my eyes. Focus.

It's not much—just a flicker of warmth in my palm, a breath of will—but it's enough. The old wards hum in recognition.

With a soft click, the chain slackens. The gate creaks open on its own.

I step inside.

The air shifts immediately. Denser. Older. The city's heartbeat dims behind me, replaced by the hush of stone and shadow.

The moon spills silver over the tops of the tombs, and the cemetery exhales around me.

The breeze picks up. Cold. Sharp. It carries the scent of old roses and fire-smoke.

I pass the tomb of the Dubois family first—it's cracked along the bottom, a spiderweb of age and flood damage blooming across the front. Someone's left a bundle of lavender tied with red twine on the step, already fading. Further in, I nod to the angel statue near the

Guidry vault, its face weather-worn and wing chipped from years of sun and salt, but still watching.

The moonlight spills across rows of the dead, casting deep shadows and glinting off coins and glass beads left as offerings. Every step I take feels known, intentional. Like retracing a dream.

And then I reach her.

Marie Laveau.

Her tomb rises like a sentinel—off-white and heavy with history, marked by chalk Xs and melted wax from generations of candlelit prayers. Roses, chicken bones, hair ties, and bottles of rum clutter the base. Offerings. Bargains. Signs of grief.

I pause, just long enough to place my fingers gently against the stone.

"Merci," I whisper. Not for anything specific. Just… for presence. For holding space.

The air around her tomb always feels different. Not threatening—watchful. Like she knows who's worthy. Who's pretending.

That's when I feel it.

The shift.

Not wind. Not imagination. Presence.

He's here.

I rise slowly, heart thundering, every nerve sparking like a match to kindling.

And then from the shadows between the tombs, a figure steps forward.

Tall. Broad-shouldered. The same face from my dream, but sharper now. Real. His eyes burn blue, the kind that sees through you. And his voice—low, velvet, dangerous—wraps around me like smoke.

"You came."

My throat goes dry. "You're real."

He steps closer, and something in my chest flares to life. The pendant on my neck grows warm—too warm.

His eyes narrow, like he's searching for something just beneath my skin. A flicker of disbelief, quickly masked. Then softly, almost as if he's afraid to ask:

"You…know me?"

The question cuts through me.

I freeze. I don't know how to answer. Because yes—but also no.

"I'm not sure," I breathe, the words rushing out in a panic before I can stop them. "I think I've had dreams of you. Or memories. They aren't clear. Just images. Feelings. But they feel real. Like they happened."

My voice climbs, tumbling out too fast now.

"How did I know you'd be here? Who are you? What is happening? Wait—so all these years, I have been feeling you watching me? What the fuck?"

The final question lands with a crack in the silence.

Even the wind pauses. And suddenly, I feel it. The spiral.

Panic curls up from the base of my spine, wrapping tightly around my lungs like a fist. My heart's thudding so hard I can hear it in my ears, feel it in my teeth. My fingers twitch like they're looking for something to hold onto, but everything around me is stone and shadow.

I try to breathe, but it comes too fast. Too shallow.

Holy fuck. Holy fuck.

I'm in a cemetery at night. With a shadowy man who knows me somehow, hopefully past stalking me. Who I've dreamed of. Felt watching me. For years.

Everything in me screams to run. To bolt back toward the gates and pretend none of this ever happened.

But I can't move.

Not yet.

Come on, Jane. Get it together.

I squeeze my eyes shut, counting backward from ten in my head— something Agatha taught me when the world feels too sharp.

Ten…nine…eight…

Breathe.

In. Out. In again.

"Okay," I whisper to myself. "Okay. You're okay. You're standing. You're breathing. You're alone—well, shit, you are not, but it's shadow-dream stalker guy—fuck it, breathe anyway."

My hands are shaking. My voice is a mess. But I'm here.

I open my eyes again. He hasn't moved.

Still watching me.

Still real.

"Jane."

Just my name.

But it hits like a slap to the face.

The sound of it in his mouth—deep, velvet, unshakably certain—rips through the panic like a blade.

Air whooshes back into my lungs. My thoughts become clearer like shattered glass snapping into place.

Suddenly, I'm here. Present. Focused.

"Alexander," I say, the name tumbling out of me as I take a shaky step backward—

—and immediately trip over something behind me.

A tumbled crystal. Left as an offering near Marie's tomb.

My heel catches. My arms flail. The world tilts.

I barely register the movement before I'm caught.

Held.

One breath, I was falling. The next, he was there.

Arms around me. Strong. Cold. Steady.

Not even a second had passed.

My heart stutters. My stomach flips. My mind connects the dots before I can argue.

Only one thing moves that fast.

A vampire.

Then suddenly—

My blood turns to fire. My stomach flips. My heart forgets its rhythm.

And then—a flash.

It's us.

Naked. Tangled in shadow and candlelight. His body driving into mine, my arms stretched back, and his hands gripping my shoulders, anchoring me to him. My head kicks back in a wave of pure pleasure, and I moan his name without shame, without fear.

It should feel like a dream. But it doesn't. It feels like a memory.

Only it's not me. Not fully.

And when he groans my name in return, it's not Jane.

"Vanessa," he moans, low and wrecked, like the word is a sacred thing on his tongue.

BAM.

I'm yanked back to the present like a door slamming shut in my chest.

But before I can think—before I can breathe—I kiss him. The vision burns through me like a truth I can't unlearn, and in that moment, kissing him feels less like a choice and more like gravity finally catching up to us.

He freezes.

Completely still.

But I don't stop.

My hands move on their own, braiding behind his neck and twisting into his hair like I've known the shape of him my whole life. Maybe longer. The passion rises like a flood, spilling over, clawing its way out of me with nowhere else to go.

I can't stop it. I can't stop myself.

He groans into the kiss.

A deep, primal sound that vibrates through my spine.

Then he moves—fast and fluid—and suddenly I'm pressed against a tomb wall, legs wrapped around his waist, his hands locked around my thighs like he'll never let me go again.

I gasp against his mouth. My static energy sparks to life, crackling under my skin like a storm breaking loose.

But he doesn't flinch. Doesn't pull away. He kisses me harder, like he's waited lifetimes for this moment and won't waste a second.

And still, he holds me like I might disappear again.

The magic intensifies.

It's not just sparks now.

It's heat. Pressure. Electricity is crawling beneath my skin like lightning searching for somewhere to land.

I feel it rising from my fingertips, licking out into the air, blue and crackling. It dances down my arms, across my chest, wrapping around us like a net of raw, burning something.

The air thickens. The tomb beneath me hums. The earth itself feels like it's holding its breath.

Alexander groans again, but this time it's different. Not just lust.

It's awe.

He pulls back slightly, just enough to rest his forehead against mine. His voice is wrecked, low, reverent.

"You're waking up."

I gasp, still clinging to him, energy still building in every inch of me.

"I—I don't know how to stop it."

My fingers twitch where they've woven into his hair. A blast of energy bursts from my palm and cracks against the tombstone behind us, leaving a glowing line along the ancient stone.

He doesn't move away. Doesn't flinch.

Instead, he closes his eyes like he's praying.

"Let it come."

My breath catches in my throat. The storm inside me surges again, like something older is clawing its way up from my bones. I feel it in my throat, in my hips, in my chest. Something unleashing.

My vision swims. Light floods behind my eyes.

I hear a name whispered on the wind—mine, but not mine.

"Velashara."

And then—

BOOM.

A pulse of energy explodes out of me.

Not painful, just pure. Radiant. Magic made flesh and memory and flame.

The cemetery lights flicker. Every candle on every tomb flares up as if in answer. Somewhere in the distance, a wrought-iron gate rattles loose in its latch.

And still he holds me.

Not afraid. Not surprised.

Only…home.

Alexander watches me in silence for a beat. Then he sets me down gently.

"I shouldn't have touched you," he says quietly. "Not before you were ready."

I glance down at my hands that are still tingling. "What am I?"

He hesitates. And that hesitation is more terrifying than anything he could've said outright.

"You're…you," he says finally, as if that should be enough. "But you're also more. Something ancient. Rewritten. Hidden."

I stare at him, not blinking. "Helpful."

He almost smiles. Almost.

"I knew you before. In another life." He swallows. "Many, actually."

"Vanessa," I whisper, the name feeling like a stone in my throat.

He nods once. "That was one of them. The one I remember at least, the most recent."

"And you were…?"

His voice drops low.

"The one they warned you about."

Goosebumps rise across my skin. "A vampire."

"A tracked one," he says quickly, gently. "I was allowed to stay from the witches' council—bound to the old magic. I was loyal. I am loyal."

"To me?"

His gaze softens, but there's fire behind it.

"Always."

I feel my knees wobble and brace myself against the tomb. The weight of it all is pressing down on me—past lives, magic, names that don't belong to me but still fit.

"I don't remember everything," he admits. "Not yet. Only fragments. Feelings. But when you touched me tonight, something shifted."

"You don't know what's happening to me?" I ask, harsher than I intend.

"I know enough to be worried for you."

He looks at me like I'm the prophecy he never believed would come true. Like I'm the key and the lock all at once.

"You're waking up. The blood moon's unlocking what was sealed. But you're not the only one who's noticed."

I frown. "Noticed?"

Before he can answer, a wind tears through the cemetery hard enough to rattle the iron gates. Somewhere behind us, a candle blows out.

And just like that, his expression darkens.

"We shouldn't be here much longer."

The wind settles again, but the air doesn't feel calm.

It feels…aware.

Alexander steps back, eyes still locked on mine.

"Get home to Agatha. Now. Don't stop. Don't talk to anyone."

My heart skips. "How do you know her?"

He doesn't answer. He just gives me one last look—something between longing and regret—then vanishes.

One blink. Gone.

Not a sound. Not a trace. Not even the crunch of gravel beneath his boots.

Just empty moonlight and the silence of the dead.

I stare at the space where he'd been, heart pounding.

"Okay," I whisper to myself, trying to catch my breath. "Hot shadow man I've apparently slept with in a past life? Vampire. Got it. Cool."

I push off the tomb, legs trembling.

"But how the hell does he know my grandma?"

I shake my head, stumbling toward the gate. "Stalker energy. Full-blown undead stalker energy."

PORTUGA
NER

CHAPTER FIVE

CANDLELIGHT CONFESSIONS

Did I listen and go straight to my gran's like he told me to?

Nope.

Of course not.

Because who the hell is he to bark orders at me like some dark, brooding hall monitor of the undead?

Yes, I kissed him. Yes, I had a literal orgasmic flashback of past-life sex under the stars or whatever the hell that was. Yes, his voice makes my bones shiver in ways I do not want to analyze right now.

But none of that gives him the right to tell me what to do.

I'm Jane. Not Vanessa. Not "reincarnated magic-mystery girl." Just Jane.

And Jane makes her own decisions—like texting her gran that I'm staying at Braelynn's and I'm "almost there" even though I am very much wandering through the Quarter half-shocked, half-feral, and about thirty seconds away from throwing my phone into the nearest gutter.

So no. Just because I put my tongue in his mouth—and maybe, maybe, wanted to put a lot more there—doesn't mean he suddenly gets to decide where I go, who I see, or how I live my life.

Get home to Agatha? Name drop much, stalker vamp? Sure. Later. Maybe.

First, I need Braelynn. And snacks. And possibly a mixed drink to scream or cry into. Or both.

I fumble with the spare key as quietly as possible because it's late, and I'm not exactly in the mood to explain why I look like I just survived a séance and a kiss from a gothic fever dream.

The door creaks open and I step inside, already halfway composing my "hey sorry I snuck in, love you, don't hate me" text—

Only to freeze.

There are voices. And not just Braelynn's.

Laughter, the clink of glasses, and someone saying the word "bitch" in a tone that could only belong to one person.

I round the corner into the kitchen, and there they are.

Fergus: lounging against the counter, broad-shouldered and grinning, a lowball glass in hand. Javi: perched dramatically on a barstool in a cropped tee and silk pants, swirling something dark and probably enchanted in a stemmed glass.

They both stop mid-sip and turn to me as I stand frozen in the doorway like I just broke into a party I wasn't invited to.

"Oh my god," I blurt out, "I wasn't expecting you to be here—I was just about to text B that I was staying in the guest room, I swear."

Fergus raises an eyebrow but doesn't move, clearly amused. Javi, however, sets his glass down slowly and glides off the stool like he's been waiting for this exact moment.

"Oh my god, you're home?" I rush forward, heart skipping a beat as I throw my arms around him. "I thought you weren't supposed to be back for another couple weeks!"

Javi hugs me tightly, warm and safe and entirely extra, then pulls back just enough to give me his signature once-over.

"Last venue had to cancel," he says, lips pursed dramatically. "Ticket sales." He rolls his eyes with theatrical flair, then winks. "So I get a couple extra weeks of vacation—and came straight home."

Then softer, his voice dipping into something more real, he says, "Couldn't get here fast enough."

He tilts his head, still holding onto my arms as he studies me.

"Something's off," he says, eyes narrowing just a fraction. "And don't try to lie, darling. You're humming like a broken crystal ball."

I let out a breath and force a crooked smile.

"It's just been a night. A lot's happening all at once. I think I'm still catching up to it."

That hangs in the air for a beat too long.

Javi's brows twitch like he wants to press further—but doesn't.

Fergus shifts where he's standing, suddenly a little more alert. He doesn't say anything, but his body language has changed—like he's on standby, just in case.

And Braelynn, seated on the couch with a drink in hand, slowly sets her glass down.

She doesn't speak right away. Just watches me with those sharp green eyes of hers—darker than mine, but just as knowing.

The air in the room shifts.

Not hostile. Not dramatic. Just changed.

The way it does when people who know you decide not to call you out.

Not yet.

"Well," Braelynn says finally, breaking the tension with a shrug. "I hope whatever it is can hold its damn horses because I just poured myself a fresh drink and put on soft pants."

"Same," Fergus mutters, raising his glass.

Javi tosses his arm around my shoulder and steers me toward the couch.

"You'll talk when you're ready," he says. "Or I'll force it out of you with wine, comfort food, and aggressive affection."

That makes me laugh. Like, actually laugh.

Which is probably why my eyes sting almost immediately after.

"I'm fine," I say softly.

And it's only partially a lie.

We all settle into the living room. Braelynn tosses me a blanket without asking. Fergus dims the overhead lights. Javi refills everyone's glasses with a flick of his wrist and the flair of someone who's mastered the art of drama and hospitality.

I curl into the corner of the couch; legs tucked under me.

"I'm sorry your tour got cut short," I say, glancing over at Javi. "That really sucks."

He waves a hand, expression softening.

"Eh, they always leave the small towns and B-markets for last just in case it happens. I knew when we hit the Carolinas that the curtain was probably coming down early."

He smiles, and this one's real.

"Besides, I'm happy to be home. This city's got better coffee, prettier witches, and my favorite people. Plus, now I get to plan your birthday!"

"Oh God," I say with an eye roll and chuckle. I've never been someone who likes to celebrate myself. I'd rather celebrate someone else.

Fergus looks over at him, voice quieter now.

"Did you…stop by your parents?"

It's not a dig. It's careful. Gentle. The kind of question you only ask someone you love.

Javi's smile fades just slightly. He doesn't get defensive, just quiet. Thoughtful.

"I got as far as the driveway," he says. "Sat there for maybe two minutes before I turned around."

Braelynn's brows furrow. I stay quiet, watching him.

"I realized they know how to reach me. If they want to, they can. But it's not up to me to cross a bridge they burned. And even if they ever do try to cross it back…"

He pauses, swirling the last of his drink before setting the glass down.

"I'm not sure I won't set it on fire. I've spent years thinking I was the problem, but I'm starting to realize maybe I was just the easiest one to blame. And maybe they don't deserve to be in my life. At least not in the version I'm building now."

The room goes still—not heavy, just full.

Fergus nods once, slow and firm. "Good."

Braelynn mutters, "Fuck toxic bridges."

I reach out and gently squeeze Javi's hand.

"You're building something beautiful. They don't get to ruin it just because they gave you the first bricks."

Javi blinks then fans himself dramatically. "Oh my god, stop. I didn't cry when I got rejected from Rupaul's Drag Race, and I won't cry now."

We all laugh—and it's the real kind. The kind that bubbles up from the chest and shakes something loose.

The laughter fades into the kind of stillness that only happens when people trust each other. The apartment hums with soft light and the clink of glassware. Javi disappears to put on a face mask. Braelynn retreats to her room with a wave and a muttered threat about no one waking her up before noon.

Fergus starts stacking the empty glasses into the sink. I hover awkwardly for a second, unsure whether to help or just go melt into the guest bed.

He glances over his shoulder.

"You holding up?"

The question's simple. But the way he asks it—low, even, no pressure—makes my throat tighten.

I nod, then shake my head, then shrug. "Honestly? I don't know."

He turns, leaning his hip against the counter, arms folded. His expression isn't pitying. It's steady. Grounded.

"You don't have to know. You just have to let people walk through it with you."

I look at him for a moment, long enough to notice the tiny scar above his eyebrow and the way his eyes always look like he's already seen the worst and decided to stay anyway.

"You're good at that," I say. "Walking with people through the mess."

Fergus smirks. "Must be the Irish in me. Generational trauma builds character."

I snort. "Should put that on a shirt."

He nods toward the hallway.

"Go sleep. We'll be here in the morning."

I pause then touch his arm briefly. Just long enough to say thank you without saying it.

And then I head down the hall toward the guest room, where I can pretend—for a few hours—that I'm just a regular girl who had a weird night and not someone with a firestorm under her skin and a vampire carved into her memories.

As I lay there, I think about the version of myself from years ago, the one who flinched when someone knocked too loudly or felt like she had to apologize for needing silence, space, clarity.

I've come so far.

I understand now that my mind isn't broken.

It's wired differently—vibrating at a higher frequency. It means I feel more, notice more, carry more. And sometimes it hurts.

But it's also beautiful.

Because I've learned how to survive my own storm.

I've learned that this brain of mine—the one that spins and spirals and sees connections others miss—comes with gifts that can't be taught.

Empathy. Creativity. Resilience. Strength.

The kind you build in silence, in struggle, in waiting, in solitude, and therapy offices and late-night breakdowns where you choose to keep going anyway.

People like me, we're needed. Deeply.

Because we see what others can't. Feel what others won't. And yes, it's harder sometimes. Because we live in layers. We don't just feel—we feel multidimensionally.

But that, too, is sacred.

And now there's a different kind of storm stirring in me. Older. Wilder.

Something sacred that doesn't quite have my name but still answers when I call.

And somewhere in the night, with my fingers curled around the cool edge of my pendant and my mind stretched too thin to settle, a single thought echoes through me like a whisper down the spine:

I'm not just waking up. I'm becoming.

I wish I could say I fell asleep peacefully, but that's not what happened.

The second my eyes closed, the heat found me.

I'm standing on something hard, splintering beneath my bare feet. The air is thick with smoke. A burning wind whips against my face.

I look up, and the sky is blood red. A full moon looms behind the smoke, swollen and watchful, as if it sees everything and offers no mercy.

Fire races toward me. I try to move, scream, fight—

—but I'm bound, and the flames are already climbing.

My chest seizes. My mouth opens. I'm burning.

I don't know if I'm screaming aloud or just inside my skull, but I jolt upright and—

Smoke.

Real smoke.

The blanket under me is singed and curling at the edges. My hands are glowing faintly, the air around them shimmering with heat.

Then—

CRASH.

The bedroom door slams open.

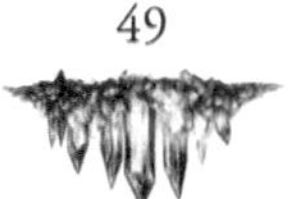

"WHAT THE FUCK!" Braelynn shouts, metal bat in hand.

Fergus storms in right behind her, barefoot and shirtless, searching the room for threats and quickly assessing the situation.

Javi follows, dramatically wrapped in a satin robe, face mask still clinging to one cheek, and clutching a half-melted palo santo stick.

"Is it demons?" he gasps. "Because I am prepared for demons."

Braelynn's eyes scan the room.

"Jesus, J," she mutters. "You're glowing."

Javi steps closer, narrowing his eyes. Then stills.

"Oh gods. That's not just a flare…"

He takes a step back, reverent now. Careful.

"It's an Ashwake."

Braelynn glances over. "The hell's an Ashwake?"

Javi doesn't answer right away. He just looks at me like I've cracked open time itself.

"It's soulfire," he says finally. "But older. Rarer. It only happens when a witch carries something ancient. Something that's waking up from another life."

His voice drops lower. Almost a whisper.

"Agatha mentioned it once when she was mentoring me— myths about it buried deep in the High Coven records. Ashwakes are supposed to be a myth. A sign of returning magic. A soul marked by prophecy."

No one speaks.

The heat in my chest pulses again.

Braelynn slowly pulls out her phone, and I glance over to see her type:

Maurice. come by tomorrow. something's wrong with J.

"We'll go see Gran in the morning," I say. "First thing." My throat is rough, my chest aching like the fire left something behind. "I need to know if there's more she hasn't told me. I can't keep pretending nothing's happening."

Fergus crosses to the bed, gently pats out the last of the scorched fabric, then cracks the window to let the smoke drift out.

"What happened?" Braelynn asks.

"I don't know," I rasp. "It felt like a dream. But deeper. Like something old."

Javi nods, softer now. "We'll figure it out together."

Fergus lingers like a quiet wall between me and everything burning. The room finally settles. Braelynn disappears and returns a few minutes later with fresh sheets and a glass of water. She strips the scorched ones quickly, silently, like she's done it a hundred times before, after setting the water down beside me.

"You need anything else?" she asks.

I shake my head.

"Want one of us to stay in here?"

I hesitate. Then: "No. It's probably safer if I'm alone."

She doesn't argue. Just nods once, presses her palm briefly to my shoulder, and leaves without another word.

The door clicks shut behind them.

For the first time since the fire, the room is quiet.

And finally—

I find darkness.

CHAPTER SIX

FIRE AND FANG

The smell of coffee pulls me from the shower like a spell of its own.

The hot water helped ease the tension in my shoulders, but my head is still a maze of fire, memory, and questions I don't know how to ask. I towel off slowly, mentally rehearsing how I'm going to tell Gran about the dream. About the fire. About the magic I can't seem to control. About him.

I step out into the living room, hair still damp, wearing a fresh pair of jeans and my vintage Midnight Margarita T-shirt from my favorite movie, Practical Magic. I am grateful that I keep a few sets of clothes here for unplanned sleepovers, or just in case. B does the same at my place, even though I don't have a spare room like she does, but my bed is big enough to share if needed. I was expecting to see just Braelynn—and instead, I walk straight into a full house. Grateful I am dressed.

Maurice is standing near the window, already nursing a mug of coffee and somehow still looking like he stepped out of a cologne ad. Beside him is a woman I've never met before, but by the look of her—short, sharp, and magnetic, with an ice-blonde bob and black roots that make her look like she could kill with a kiss—has to be Kaia. She's studying the room like she's casing it.

Fergus and Javi are in the kitchen, half-dressed and sipping coffee like they've lived here for years. Javi is in silk pajamas with a satin head wrap and no shame. Fergus has one sock on and is growling at the coffee pot like it insulted his mother.

"Jane," Maurice says gently, like he's been waiting for me to appear. "This is Kaia."

Kaia nods with an amused smirk. "So you're the one sparking like a live wire in your sleep."

Before I can respond, the front door opens again and Braelynn walks in, arms full of fresh flowers.

"Hey, hey," she says, beaming. "I stopped by Wild Bloom really quick and threw this together for you."

She owns the place—a flower shop she built from the ground up. Every stem she touches hums with intention.

She crosses the room and hands me the bouquet—lavender, rosemary, white peonies, and a few stems I don't recognize but instantly feel. A soft hum seems to radiate from the blooms.

"These'll help with calming and grounding," B says casually, like she just brought me a latte and not an enchanted armful of Earth-magic.

I blink, touched. "Thanks, B. They're beautiful."

Kaia arches a brow, arms crossed. "Grounding, huh? Sounds pretty witchy for a wolf."

Braelynn rolls her eyes. "It's called Pinterest. Calm down."

Kaia smirks but doesn't push it.

Then she turns to B. "By the way, your dad wants to see you before we head to Jane's grandmother's. Something about changes to night patrols."

Braelynn's entire posture shifts. "Seriously? Right now?"

Kaia shrugs. "His words. I'm just the messenger."

I glance around the room, confusion sinking in. "Wait. Everyone's coming to Gran's? I thought it was just going to be me and B working at the shop. I'm not sure there's enough food."

Maurice grins. "Is she making gumbo?"

Just then, my phone buzzes. A text from Gran:

I made enough for everyone. Don't worry. See you all soon. Love, Gran. PS: Tell Javi to bring that sweet red he's been saving. Both bottles.

I let out a soft laugh. "Never mind. Gran says we're all set. And Javi—she wants both bottles."

Javi groans from the kitchen. "Of course she does. That woman is a menace. Fine. I'll grab them on the way. And I'll need at least an hour to de-glitter. You're welcome."

Fergus pours himself a second cup. "I'll stop by the bar and grab dessert. Beignets okay?"

"Beignets are always okay," Braelynn says.

As the room starts to bustle with people finishing coffee and gathering their things, it's clear we're splitting up for now. Javi and Fergus will meet us at Gran's. That leaves me, B, Maurice, and Kaia walking to B's place so she can talk to her dad.

The air outside is hot and thick, New Orleans in her summer skin. The kind that clings.

Kaia walks beside Braelynn with a casual confidence, her shoulder just barely brushing B's as they move. She tosses a comment over her shoulder. "You always give people lavender when they're stressed?"

Braelynn rolls her eyes. "Only the ones who scream in their sleep and accidentally set things on fire."

Kaia smirks. "Noted."

Maurice slows his pace and gently touches my arm. "Hey," he says softly. "Are you okay?"

I don't answer at first. I just let the question sit between us for a few beats. Finally, I shake my head. "Not really. But I don't know how to explain it yet. It's like something's trying to wake up inside me, and every time I get close to understanding it, it slips away."

He looks at me like he already understands. "You don't have to explain it all. Just don't carry it alone."

That undoes me a little. There's something in Maurice's voice—calm and steady—that feels like the ground I've been missing.

As we turn the corner toward Braelynn's building, a new heaviness settles in my stomach.

Braelynn's father.

I've known him for years. Seen him at full moons, patrol briefings, and the occasional pack event. He's never said anything cruel to me, but he's never shown warmth, either. Always watching me with that same tight-lipped expression, like I'm a question he doesn't want the answer to.

I used to think he just didn't like outsiders. But lately, I wonder if it's something else. If he resents how close I am to B. If he thinks I've encouraged her to drift from her duties, to question the rigid structures he's built his life around.

Maybe I did.

Maybe that's exactly what he sees every time he looks at me.

I don't know what's waiting for us behind that door.

But I know the air's about to shift again.

We reach the side door of Braelynn's father's compound—a two-story stone building nestled behind wrought-iron gates on the edge of the Bywater. It looks more like a historical estate than a private home, with thick shutters and a courtyard that smells faintly of tobacco and cypress.

Braelynn hesitates for a second before knocking, her jaw tight. She doesn't need to say it—I already know this isn't her favorite place.

The door opens before her knuckles land.

Standing in the doorway is Packmaster Samuel Delacroix—broad-shouldered, silver-haired, and coldly imposing. His chiseled features and storm-gray eyes give him a wolfish kind of stillness—the kind that watches, calculates, waits. He wears a weathered black leather jacket over dark clothes, more militant than fatherly, and carries an air of practiced authority that makes every word feel like an order. There's a hardness to him that feels like it's always been there—but something deeper, too. A grief that never thawed.

His gaze sweeps the group before settling on Braelynn.

"You're late."

B folds her arms. "Wasn't told I was expected."

"You are now," he says flatly, stepping back to let us in. "Maurice."

"Uncle," Maurice nods, respectful but not warm.

There's a beat of tension before Kaia strides in after us, completely unfazed.

Inside, the air is cooler but heavier.

I hang back near the doorway as Braelynn and her father start talking in low tones. Maurice stays beside me, and Kaia leans against a stone pillar like she's ready for this to be over.

"You're being reassigned," Samuel says bluntly to Braelynn. "Kaia is joining night patrol. She'll be your second. You're expected to train her on routes, alert codes, and the chain-of-command procedure. No improvising."

Braelynn's brows rise. "She's not new."

"She's not trained in this pack," he replies without blinking.

Kaia crosses her arms. "I don't need a babysitter."

Samuel turns toward her slowly, his tone sharpening. "And I don't need lip from a stray with no rank and a history of defiance."

Kaia's eyes don't flicker. "My last alpha thought the only place for a woman was beneath him. I left. I'm not here to roll over for another man who confuses control with leadership."

His jaw tightens. "Watch yourself."

"I always do."

It's a standoff. One she doesn't lose.

I glance at Braelynn, who's biting her bottom lip, but her eyes are gleaming. There's a flicker of something I recognize—satisfaction. Kaia just said what B's been swallowing for years.

"Get her up to speed," Samuel growls at Braelynn before turning on his heel and disappearing deeper into the house.

The moment the door clicks shut behind him, the tension drains like someone let the air out of the room.

Kaia exhales through her nose. "He's a ray of goddamn sunshine."

Braelynn lets out a breathy laugh and shakes her head. "You've got nerve, I'll give you that."

Kaia smirks. "I've got scars to match."

B hesitates, then adds, "Thanks for standing your ground."

Kaia shrugs. "Not the first alpha who's tried to put me in a cage. Won't be the last."

Braelynn's voice softens. "Can you cover the shift tonight if I need to stay longer with Jane and Gran?"

Kaia nods without hesitation. "Yeah. I got you."

For a second, neither of them says anything. But something unspoken passes between them. A truce. Maybe the beginning of something else.

Unlike witches or vampires, there is no central High Council for wolves. Each pack is sovereign—ruled by a Packmaster and their chosen Second. Their word is law in their territory. No one else interferes. Ever. Pack Masters may talk. They may trade. But they don't rule each other. Crossing that line? It's considered a challenge. An insult. Which makes Kaia's pushback today…bold. Maybe even dangerous.

As we step back out into the sticky New Orleans air, I glance over at Maurice, then back at the building behind us.

I've known that man—Samuel Delacroix—since I was a kid. After the storm, when Katrina took both Braelynn's mom Celeste and Maurice's parents, Samuel took Maurice in and raised him alongside B. Raised them under the same roof. But he never let Maurice forget who made the rules. I think he is threatened by him.

Now I see it more clearly. Samuel doesn't dislike me because I'm weak. He resents that I help give Braelynn something he can't control. Freedom. Distance. A mind of her own.

CHAPTER SEVEN

ASHWAKE AND SUNDRY

The closer we get to Séance & Sundry, the tighter my chest feels.

Call it avoidant, call it non-confrontational—I don't care. All I know is that when something this emotionally heavy lands on my shoulders, my brain kicks into overdrive. I script the whole conversation in my head before it even happens. The questions. The answers I hope to get. The reactions I'm afraid of.

And when it's too much—when the weight of it all starts pressing down—I want to check out. Disassociate. Crawl under a blanket and put on a comfort show like Friends I've seen a hundred times or reread a book I already know the ending to. Something predictable. Something safe. Something that lets me slip out of my skin for a while and just be somewhere else.

But today? I don't have the luxury of pre-planning or escaping. Because the conversation we're about to have isn't just personal.

It's about me.

And magic.

And something ancient clawing its way to the surface.

It's about all eyes on me—and not knowing what the hell they'll see when they look too closely.

I glance over and see B walking beside me, stiff and quiet, clearly caught in her own head.

Just as I'm about to say something, Maurice nudges me gently and lowers his voice.

"Hey," he says. "How are you holding up?"

I shrug. "I guess we'll find out soon."

He gives me a soft smile, but there's something sharper behind it—something knowing. Then his nostrils flare slightly. He tilts his head and looks at me again.

"Wait—what are you wearing? You smell really good today."

I blink. "Random much?"

He laughs. "I'm just saying, for someone who had nightmares about burning alive and scorched half the bed, you look kinda radiant. And you smell amazing."

My cheeks flush. My heart does that annoying flutter thing.

He always knows how to pull me back into the moment—how to say the exact thing I didn't know I needed to hear. It's unfair.

I roll my eyes and say, "I used whatever was in the bathroom. Maybe I should bottle it and sell it as 'trauma chic.'"

He chuckles again. "You should. I'd buy it."

We walk in silence for a few beats before I glance over at B again. Still quiet. Still stiff.

I decide to poke the bear.

"So, Kaia's really nice, huh?" I say, as casually as possible. "And brave. And ballsy."

B smirks. "I told you she was cool."

"Yeah," I say, wagging my brows. "But you didn't tell me she was hot and that the two of you have enough chemistry to ignite another fire."

Braelynn gives me a look. "Seriously? How are you even thinking about that right now?"

"Because I'm gifted," I deadpan. "And also, because I was there. She was not looking at you like you're some Packmaster's daughter. She was looking at you like she wanted to stay."

B scoffs, but there's the faintest flush on her cheeks. "She was just being nice."

"Mm-hmm."

She gives me a slight side-eye and then falls quiet again, eyes clouding over like the earlier softness never happened.

I let it drop. For now.

But the silence between us doesn't feel empty—it feels like the kind that knows a storm is coming.

The wrought-iron sign above the door reads Séance & Sundry, its letters carved in a soft curve, weathered by time but lovingly maintained. Vines twist around the post, half in bloom, and an old broom leans casually by the stoop like it's been there for centuries. The shutters are painted a dusty lavender, and the glass windowpanes shimmer faintly even in daylight—like they remember moonlight better than sun.

The second we open the door, a vintage bell above the frame jingles with a sound so precise it feels intentional—like it's announcing us, specifically.

Inside, the scent hits immediately: warm beeswax, herbs, cedar smoke, and just the faintest undertone of rose and old paper. There are shelves of crystals and dried bundles hanging upside down near the windows. The counter holds a copper cash box, a polished black mirror, and a feather quill that sometimes writes on its own when Agatha's not looking. It smells like magic in here. But also…home.

B breathes in deep and mutters, "Damn. Gran's gumbo is already making me emotional."

Maurice lifts a brow and sniffs the air. "Wait, is that duck and andouille?"

"You know it is," B says. "That's her 'company's coming' gumbo. She made it upstairs in the apartment."

He lets out a low whistle. "Guess we made the guest list after all."

Before I can laugh, I hear the familiar sound of soft slippers on old wood and the voice that has anchored me since I was a child.

"There y'all are," Gran says, appearing at the top of the stairwell in a swirl of woven skirts and candlelight. "I was starting to worry the city had swallowed you whole."

My Gran, Agatha Fontenot, is seventy-three years old and effortlessly ageless. She wears layered shawls, long skirts, and stacks of silver rings that click gently when she moves. Her gray hair is piled into a loose twist with silver pins. Her green eyes—same as mine, but sharper—crinkle with warmth the moment she sees us. And her presence, as always, feels like safety.

I don't realize I'm moving until I'm already in her arms.

She holds me close and tight, the kind of hug that says everything without asking anything. Her voice drops to a whisper just for me. "My sweet Janey. Don't worry, sweetheart. It's all going to be okay."

Something unknots in my chest.

Braelynn is right behind me and wraps her arms around Gran from the other side. "Hi, Gran," she says, burying her face into her shoulder like she's a teenager again.

Maurice follows, pulling Gran into a side hug and kissing her cheek. "Hey, Aggie."

She swats at him affectionately. "Don't you go trying to sweet-talk me for seconds."

"I don't need to." He grins. "You always make too much."

The front door jingles again just in time for Javi to sweep in like he's making an entrance at the Met Gala. He's in a sheer black duster and combat boots, holding two bottles of red wine in one arm and a candle in the other.

"I have arrived," he announces. "With libations and good intentions."

Gran claps her hands once. "There he is. I was just thinking about you, sugar."

"I know. I felt it," Javi says with a wink.

I always tell people Javi is all spice, but the truth is he's got more sugar than anyone I know. He carries himself well, glittered edges and sass that could cut glass, but underneath he's the kind of soul that makes you believe in gentleness again. He's multidimensional in the most beautiful ways.

I can't help but laugh remembering the night at Fergus's bar when some drunk redneck decided he didn't like the look of a man in eyeliner. He swung at Javi—big mistake. Javi took him down so fast the guy didn't even realize he was on the floor until the whole room was staring. The look on his face when he realized the man who floored him was the same one he'd just mocked for wearing eyeshadow? That image is seared into my memory, and I'll probably laugh about it until the day I die.

But that's the thing about Javi—he can be fire when he needs to be, but he's also soft when it matters most. I remember once before a date, I broke down because I didn't know what to wear, if I should change my makeup, or if I even belonged in the whole mess of romance. He sat me down, brushed the hair back from my face, and reminded me that I was enough—that I didn't need to reinvent myself for anyone. That night, he held me together in ways I didn't even realize I was falling apart.

Maybe that's why Gran loves him so much. He's got that same nurturing soul as her, steady and patient. No surprise the two of them have taken to mentoring young witches together. Javi might sparkle with spice, but the sugar runs deep—and it's what makes him family.

Fergus is right behind him, quieter, holding a small brown paper bag in one hand and a bottle in the other. "Hope you saved me a spot," he says.

Agatha grins. "For you, always."

Fergus hands over the bag. "Packed a couple extra beignets just for you—and a little scotch, for the long days when wine just won't cut it."

Agatha gives him a pleased hum. "Lord, you boys do know how to spoil an old woman."

Fergus has this way of scanning a room, like a sidelined protector—always observant, always aware of what energy was shifting. It makes me feel safer without even realizing I need to. But I know better than to mistake his quiet for distance.

With Fergus, depth ran like a river just under the surface. I think about the night we ended up on FaceTime, both of us restless at two in the morning. He'd leaned against the headboard, hair mussed, voice low as he admitted he was interested in someone but didn't know how to proceed. For all his size and steady strength, he'd been vulnerable. Soft. It made me trust him enough to confide too, to admit I'd been wrestling with feelings about Maurice—how sometimes I thought of him in ways that scared me.

Fergus had tilted his head, thoughtful, then grinned in that crooked, boyish way of his. "I love the idea," he'd said, "but just be sure, Jane. You don't want to tangle yourself in a knot you can't undo. Still—hell, it feels right, but I am the biased friend." He'd winked, holding up his hand to the camera until I laughed and lifted mine. "Pinky promise," he said solemnly. "Not a word to anyone." That is Fergus: the man who keeps the world steady in small, unseen ways, and somehow makes you braver just by letting you know he is in your corner.

As if it's the most natural thing in the world, we all start to move together toward the back stairs that lead up to Gran's apartment. It's a warm, narrow hallway that smells like cinnamon and clove. The walls are lined with old photographs, and at the top is a curtained archway that opens into her home.

The apartment above Séance & Sundry is even more magical than the shop below. Windows framed in lace and ivy. A crooked dining table that's been charmed to always feel like it fits just enough. Candles already flicker in the chandelier—lit by a flick of Agatha's fingers as we enter. There's a warmth here that sinks into the bones.

We all fall into our rhythm: Braelynn uncorks the wine, Javi arranges a side platter of bread and cheese with unnecessary flair. Fergus sets the beignets out on a cooling rack by the window. Maurice checks on the gumbo pot like he's earned the right.

And me?

I just stand there for a moment, taking it all in.

The scent of sage and duck and rosemary fills the space. The sound of my people—their laughter, their teasing, the way they move together like this is their second home. Gran has a way of making her place feel like home to anyone who walks through the door. For B and Maurice, it's been that way since we were teenagers—her kitchen their second home long before Javi and Fergus found their seats at the table in our twenties.

Agatha waves her hand, and the last few candles flicker to life.

"Alright," she says, smiling. "Let's eat before this gumbo hexes us all for ignoring it."

And just like that, we're gathered.

Not just for dinner.

But for answers.

After dinner, the table doesn't empty right away.

Dessert makes its rounds—powdered beignets dusting the air like magic, paired with a smooth red that Javi claims could charm secrets from a ghost. Laughter blooms, not forced but easy, and for a while, it feels like we're just people. Not witches or wolves or reincarnated souls with fire in our veins.

The sky outside deepens to indigo. The air shifts, and I feel the hum of night settling in, brushing against the windows like a whisper. Something is coming. We all feel it.

The energy shifts again.

Gran clears her throat, looking directly at me. "Janey," she says, voice soft but firm. "It's time we talk."

The wine is half-drunk. The candles burn low. But the room—our people—falls silent with one glance from her.

She folds her hands on the table. Her voice lowers.

"This is what I've been able to gather," she begins, "from what I was told growing up in our line, the old grimoires, and my own research once I realized something deeper was happening."

She pauses, scanning our faces.

"There was an ancient witch. No one remembers her first name now—only her power and her fate. She fell in love with a being from the Eternal Realm who snuck into our realm through a larger portal gate curious to take a look around. But not just any creature, something old, something powerful. Magic of fire pulsed through him, but to fit in here he shifted into human form. And though they came from different worlds, he loved her back."

Agatha leans back slightly, the candlelight softening her features.

"She was already strong—one of the most gifted in our known bloodline—but their union made her even stronger. She was said to hold the powers of the sky—what we now understand was lightning. She became pregnant and gave birth to a daughter, a child who carried the fire of the Eternal and the sky-wrought magic of the witch. The first of our line. Her last name was Velashara."

Javi lets out a quiet breath.

Agatha continues. "Before she died, that witch recorded a prophecy in her grimoire. Most of it is still lost, but the part that survived—the part I was taught—is this: that the line would continue through daughters, all women, until your father, Janey. And that one day, her soul would return in the daughter of a son. The one would be born of a man."

My pulse thunders in my ears.

Gran looks at all of us now. "As you know, a couple hundred years ago, a pact was formed between witches and wolves. Together, we banished most of the vampires to the Eternal Realm—because unlike us, who are born and die, vampires were created by turning others. That wasn't nature. That was invasion. To make matters worse, some had what was called Blood Lust and couldn't control their feeding."

She sips her wine before continuing.

"Some vampires sided with us. Those were marked by high witches and seers. To be watched if they stayed in our realm. Contained. But others resisted. They vanished—some captured, some fought, and some were dragged back into the Eternal Realm, which was sealed. Not permanently, though. Just…paused. Contained. That realm is full of immortal creatures. Magic that warps reality. And we've never figured out how to close the gate for good."

Javi's expression grows tense.

Agatha sets her glass down.

"The witch who helped seal it—our witch—was betrayed and captured. Burned at the stake. Her vampire lover arrived too late. They thought her line ended that night."

She exhales.

"But it didn't."

"Because she had a sibling," I whisper, barely finding my voice.

Agatha nods. "A sibling she never knew. The line continued in secret, taking the name Fontenot. That's our name now. Mine. Yours. But the full power of the magic didn't disappear. It went quiet. Hidden."

She turns to me fully. "Something has always veiled this history from my sight. And that alone tells me it's more powerful than I imagined. I didn't tell you sooner because I hoped I could uncover more first. I thought I had time."

Her fingers tighten around a folded piece of parchment.

"But I don't think we do anymore. The blood moon is coming. And I believe it holds meaning—maybe even a trigger—but I don't know what."

She stands and walks toward me.

"There's a vault," she says. "Beneath St. Louis Cathedral. Hidden deep under stone and spell. It was designed to open only for the returned soul of the first Velashara."

My breath catches.

"I believe that's you, Janey."

She presses the parchment into my hand.

"You're going to need to unlock it."

CHAPTER EIGHT

BENEATH THE STONE

Gran doesn't come with us.

She walks us to the shop's back entrance, her shawl wrapped tightly around her shoulders despite the lingering heat in the air. The streetlamp above casts a soft gold light across her face, and for the first time in a long time, she looks tired.

"There's a reason I'm not going with you," she says, her voice low but steady. "I've tried before, years ago. The vault wouldn't let me in. I could sense it—old magic that was waiting for something…someone. It never opened for me."

She reaches for my hand and presses it gently. "But you? It's been waiting for you." She holds my gaze, her voice dipping lower. "The wards placed by the High Council on the exterior of the vault wore off long ago—forgotten, like the texts and grimoires it guards. But the inner gate, the spells woven into the stone itself, those are still intact. That's where you come in. I believe they'll open for you."

I swallow hard and nod, unsure what to say. My throat is already tight.

"Be safe," she adds. "Stay together."

And with that, she steps back into the shadows of Séance & Sundry, leaving us to the night.

The streets of the French Quarter feel different now.

Quieter. Heavier.

Even the usual hum of music and drunken laughter seems to hold its breath as we head toward St. Louis Cathedral. Six shadows moving with purpose through the city's haunted heart.

The air is thick with jasmine and river wind, damp stone and summer secrets. Moonlight flickers between the iron balconies, and every footstep echoes just a little too loudly.

I walk in silence, tucked between B and Maurice.

But inside, I'm a mess.

I know I should've said more. About the dream. The fire. About the way the flames didn't just surround me—they consumed me. How I woke up tasting ash and feeling like something inside me had cracked open. The blood moon burning red in the sky like some kind of omen. Maybe that is what tied us together in fate. Maybe it is what sealed my magic until its return.

And I should've mentioned the part where I kissed a vampire in the cemetery the other night. A vampire who, according to Gran's story and my dreams, may have been my lover in a past life.

But I didn't.

I couldn't.

It was all too much, too fast. I barely had time to process what Agatha told me, let alone throw Alexander and our spontaneous undead make-out session into the mix.

And if I'm honest…

There's still a part of me that wonders if it even happened.

The way the air shifted. The pull between us. The spark when we touched. It felt real—but so do dreams sometimes. So do warnings.

I glance ahead. The cathedral looms closer, framed by clouds and moonlight like it's been waiting for us.

And maybe it has.

We slip through the back courtyard, our footsteps muffled by cracked stones and patches of overgrown ferns. The air hangs heavy with moisture, and moss drips from the wrought-iron fence like green lace.

Fergus takes point without needing to be asked. Javi is beside me, quiet for once, a steady presence just behind Braelynn and Maurice. We move like a pulse—each of us carrying our own tension, our own questions.

B glances back at me. "You sure about this?"

"No," I say honestly. "But I don't think it's about being sure."

She nods once. That's all we need.

The entrance to the underground passage is behind the old tomb in the far corner of the cathedral's shadow. Most wouldn't notice the sigil carved into the stone base: faded, water-worn, half-covered in ivy.

But my hand finds it without hesitation. It's warm.

A shiver runs through my spine as the sigil pulses beneath my palm. The stone groans, then shifts, grating open with a reluctant kind of sigh. Cold air rushes up from below.

Javi whistles low under his breath. "Well damn. Guess we're really doing this."

We descend one by one into the darkness.

The air down here is colder, damp, almost humming. The stone walls sweat with age. Our lanterns flicker, casting shadows that dance across the narrow path.

Braelynn mutters, "This feels like the start of every horror movie I swore I'd never die in."

Maurice's hand brushes against hers. "You won't. You've got me."

Javi snorts. "Oh good. Our odds just went up to 'slightly less than doomed.'"

Despite myself, I laugh. Quiet, breathy. Grateful.

The hallway opens suddenly, like the ribcage of the world cracking apart.

We step into a chamber carved deep into the bones of the city. Stalactites hang from the ceiling like teeth. The stone glows faintly, veins of quartz catching the lantern light in soft, iridescent streaks.

The space is circular. No windows. No sound. But not empty.

Shelves line the curved walls, overflowing with ancient texts, crumbling scrolls, and leather-bound tomes etched in languages I don't recognize. Some pulse faintly with residual magic. Some feel wrong to look at for too long.

As we cross the threshold, the iron sconces along the wall ignite one by one, casting the room in golden, flickering light.

But it's more than fire.

Each flame spirals outward before settling, curling into smoky symbols that hover midair before fading. Glyphs. Not just light. Memory.

Fergus inhales sharply. "What the hell kind of magic is this?"

"Old," Javi answers, his voice barely above a whisper. "The kind that remembers being forgotten."

But I'm not watching the fire.

I feel a pull.

Like a thread between my ribs tugging forward. A whisper too soft to catch, but insistent. Warmth spreads across my skin—not from the flames, but from something older. Deeper.

I follow it.

My footsteps don't echo like the others. The air around me thickens, then clears, as if the room is adjusting to me.

I pause near a warped shelf lined with brittle parchment and forgotten bindings. My fingers hover above the spines.

That one.

The thought isn't mine. But it's in my head, steady and sure.

I reach out.

A seam in the stone. Barely visible. I press it.

A hidden panel slides open with a soft click, revealing a compartment wrapped in shadow. Inside, resting on a velvet-lined cradle, is a book.

The grimoire.

The grimoire was bound in a material that shifted between shadow and sheen, its surface traced with fine filagree that shimmered like starlight trapped in ink. Cool to the touch and alive with humming energy. It feels familiar. Like it's remembering me.

I reach for it—the moment my fingers graze the surface, something slams through me.

Flashes.

A woman with white hair, screaming through fire. A dragon rising behind her, wings unfurling like smoke and flame. The sensation of wings beneath my own skin. A man with dark eyes cradling her as she bleeds, whispering her name. Wait, whispering MY name. Suddenly I am behind her eyes, no longer watching.

"Lyriën Velashara."

The voice coils around me like smoke. A memory I never made.

And then another whisper, softer but sharper, written into my bones:

Born of a man under a sky of fire, she came. Here once before and back to reclaim.

I stumble back.

The grimoire stays locked tight in my hands—its clasp unmoving despite the glow pulsing beneath its cover. The warmth fades, but the memory lingers like smoke on my skin.

Maurice is there instantly, hand steady at my elbow. "What happened?"

I blink, disoriented. "It's sealed. But it knew me. It said my, I mean, her name."

B moves closer, eyes narrowed with concern. "What name, J?"

I hesitate, throat dry.

Then, softly: "Lyriën Velashara."

Silence floods the chamber.

Fergus stills and Javi shifts behind me. "That name's not in any of the Council's records. Not in any we've ever seen."

Javi leans forward slightly, voice low. "But the book knew it and Gran mentioned Velashara. That means it's real."

And somewhere in the flickering dark, the past begins to stir.

Chartres

CHAPTER NINE

STORMSONG AND SMOKE

Three days slipped by in a blur—me, the grimoire, and a whole lot of unanswered questions.

Three days of whispered translations, failed unlocking spells, and Javi cross-referencing ancient glyphs until his eyeliner smudged into war paint. Gran's kept mostly quiet—her brows in a constant furrow, her fingers trailing over her herb jars and half-finished sigils like she's trying to remember something her bones forgot.

I've tried everything to open it—candles, salt circles, even whispering every spell Gran ever taught me. Nothing. The pages stay locked, the cover cold as stone, like it's waiting for something I don't have yet. Nothing.

While we've been stuck pouring over dusty pages and faded records, B, Maurice, and Fergus have been up to their ears in pack patrols. There were two confirmed sightings of unmarked vampires in the Quarter—rogue ones, not sanctioned by the High Council. Which, of course, has Samuel Delacroix acting even more insufferable than usual. Grislier, B called it. Like someone replaced her father with a meat cleaver and bad attitude.

The shop's closed today—it always is on Mondays and Tuesdays. Gran's out running her usual errands, and Javi's off poking around the more accessible Council members for answers. If Gran went herself, it'd raise too many red flags.

So for once, I'm alone. And honestly? I don't hate it.

The storm rolled in just after noon, and it hasn't let up. A soft, steady rain kisses the wrought-iron balcony rail, thunder curling lazily through the sky. Both sets of French doors off my balcony are wide open, letting in the rhythmic patter and the clean, wild scent of magnolias soaked in summer rain.

The floor-length sheer white curtains drift in the breeze like ghosts. Inside, my apartment glows soft and golden—candlelight flickering against old brick, the occasional gust making the flames dance like they're laughing with me.

I'm curled up beneath my favorite blanket, still warm from my earlier shower. Today's a satin robe day. Blush pink, like the seamless panties beneath it—cute but comfortable, the kind that don't ride or dig or remind you of their existence every time you breathe. Honestly, I'd go commando if I didn't think the robe might betray me with the slightest shift.

Kindergarten Cop plays quietly on my laptop, tucked into the curve of my legs.

Yes, that Kindergarten Cop. And before you ask me why—well, why not? It's hilarious. And besides, it makes me laugh because Maurice is, believe it or not, a kindergarten teacher.

Big bad wolf by night. Giant teddy bear by day.

His kids adore him. I've seen it. If they spot him in public, they demand their parents stop so they can sprint over, arms outstretched, ready to tackle him with hugs and sticky high-fives. One time I saw a toddler collapse in sobs because Maurice had to leave, and she hadn't finished telling him about her glitter bug collection.

Seeing him with little ones could melt the heart of even the coldest immortal. The credits roll.

I close my laptop and set it gently to the side, sinking deeper into the cocoon of warm blankets and soft light. The storm outside doesn't let up—it pulses steady and slow, a heartbeat of rain tapping against the iron balcony rails like it's keeping time just for me. I exhale, content. For a moment, everything is still. But stillness is dangerous. Because the second I let go, he slips back in.

Alexander.

I've thought about him constantly since that night in the cemetery—since his voice poured into my bones like something remembered, something mine. I haven't seen him. Haven't heard a single whisper or felt that haunting, ancient presence nearby. But gods, I feel him.

Like he branded himself into me with one stolen kiss and the brush of his body against mine. There's something in the way he looked at me, like he was memorizing a song I've already forgotten. It stirs something old and restless in me, but I don't know if it's love, fate, or just a trick of memory. Part of me wants to reach for it, and part of me wants to run before it burns me alive.

The memory rises uninvited—the weight of him between my thighs, the way my magic sparked at his touch. The heat in his eyes. The ache he left behind.

My breath catches as the image deepens, darkens. What if he hadn't stopped it?

What if he had slid inside me—slowly, inch by inch, with that same reverent hunger in his gaze? What if I had felt every trembling stretch, every inch of him claiming me like I was already his? My cheeks burn as the fantasy unfurls, heat curling low in my belly. I imagine the sound of his moan—low, guttural, caught between our mouths as he kissed me through it.

I imagine him whispering my name against my throat. Like it was sacred. Like he needed it.

My thighs press together, breath shallow. My fingers twitch beneath the blankets.

My hand wants to wander again.

Just then, a knock. I jolt like I've been shocked, practically leaping out of my skin. My heart slams into my ribs, breath catching in my throat as the fantasy shatters and I stare toward the front door, irritated by the disruption.

What the hell?

It's barely three. No deliveries. No appointments. Javi would've texted. Gran's out. B's on patrol. Who the—I wrap my robe a little tighter and pad barefoot to the door. I unlock it and pull it open—

And for a second, I genuinely wonder if I've fallen asleep midday and my dream is staging a very cruel encore.

Because it's him.

Alexander leans against the doorframe like sin dressed in confidence, one hand tucked into the pocket of his black dress slacks, matching his belt and button-down also classic black. Go figure. Vampire in all black. I almost laugh to myself before seeing his head tilted just enough to look both curious and sure of himself. He is annoyingly exquisite. He's wearing that cocky, slow-burn smirk, like he knows exactly what I was thinking about before he knocked.

Which, unfortunately, he probably does.

How is it possible for someone to look so hungry, so seductive, and still feel like warmth creeping through a long-forgotten place in your chest?

Is this a vampire thing? Is this how they lure prey?

Or is it something else? Something older. Something that remembers.

He meets my gaze with those dark ocean eyes and says, voice like velvet and thunder, "May I come in?"

I blink. "What, like in the movies? You need an invitation?"

He laughs—a low, easy sound—and steps inside without waiting for permission. Not rudely. Not forcefully. Just effortlessly. Like he knows I'd already decided the second I saw him.

I shut the door behind him and suddenly become painfully aware of what I'm wearing. And worse, what I'm not wearing.

Fuck my life.

He takes in the room slowly—candlelit corners, storm-drenched balcony, the way the sheer curtains dance in the breeze like whispers.

"This is quite the scene you've set," he murmurs, eyes drifting over me like smoke. "What are you doing all alone in here, wrapped in satin and candlelight?"

I scoff, trying to cover the flush rising in my cheeks. "Nothing you need to worry about."

But he's already moving—that slow, predatory saunter, like he's tracking something that already belongs to him. His presence fills the room before he even touches me.

Then he does.

Just his fingertips. Pressed to my belly, light as breath.

He walks me backward with nothing but that touch, and I let him, until my back hits the wall with a soft thud and my breath escapes in a shiver.

Heat. Rising.

His eyes—God, his eyes. That impossible blue, dark as the ocean on a moonless night. His hair is damp at the ends like he's been caught in the storm, and he smells like wet cedar, danger, and memory. I want to breathe him in until I forget my own name.

I glance at his mouth.

Soft. Perfect. Sin incarnate.

He catches me looking and smirks slow and devious, like he's already undressed every thought I've ever had about him.

He leans in, his voice a velvet rasp against my ear. "I've touched myself thinking of you," he whispers, reverent and wrecked. "Have you thought of me while you made yourself come? Were you just about to do it again?"

Before I can answer—before I can even breathe—his fingertips slip beneath the edge of my robe. Slow. Intentional. Like he already knows the answer.

They trace the curve of my hip, brushing the damp silk of my panties—right where I ache for him most.

I inhale sharply, knees trembling.

His voice dips, dark silk and hunger. "Thought so."

I feel him in the pit of my stomach, in the heat between my legs, in the space behind my ribs where breath forgets how to move. My fingers twitch at my sides, torn between pushing him away and pulling him closer.

He decides for me.

Alexander leans in and kisses me—no warning, no hesitation, just a claiming. It's fire and hunger and every unfinished sentence between us.

His lips part mine like a secret, tongue teasing, coaxing. One hand cradles my cheek. The other settles low at my waist, fingers slipping under the robe again, brushing my heat.

My knees weaken instantly. I cling to him, fingers curling into his shirt like he might vanish if I let go.

But he doesn't vanish.

He presses.

His body molds to mine, hard and unrelenting, the thick length of him nestled between my thighs where my robe has parted. I gasp into his mouth, and he swallows it—grinding with slow, torturous friction that makes me moan.

He breaks the kiss just enough to breathe against my lips, "I've dreamed of this. Of you. Every night since I touched you."

I pull him back, greedy and unafraid, tasting that truth on his tongue—something ancient and burning and alive.

We stumble toward the bed, not laughing, not speaking—devouring. The candlelight flares as he guides me backward until the backs of my knees hit the mattress.

He steps back just far enough to see me—really see me. And when my robe begins to slip, his gaze darkens like a sky before lightning.

"Take it off," he says, voice low and commanding.

I let it fall.

It slides down the curves of my body and pools at my feet like rosewater, and I'm left in nothing but blush-pink panties and candlelight. His eyes rake over me, slow, reverent, ruined.

"You're perfect," he murmurs.

Then he strips.

Shirt first, ripping his buttons and removing faster than I can register the movement, then his belt with one hand, so fast it cracks in the air with the force of him pulling it out of the loops, revealing a body carved from centuries of survival and longing. Lean, powerful, every inch a contradiction of grace and brutality. Then pants and boxers, until he stands before me, bare and unashamed.

My breath stutters.

Every part of him is poetry—taut muscle, thick cock, and the kind of hunger that doesn't just burn. It consumes.

Then he's on me again.

Lips at my collarbone. Teeth grazing my breast. Fingers hooking my panties and dragging them down slowly. Deliberate. Torturous.

Until I'm bare beneath him.

Open. Waiting. His.

He kisses down my body like he's chasing a memory he was never allowed to touch. Worshipful. Desperate. Controlled only by the depth of his need.

"Are you wet for me?" he whispers, voice dragging along my skin.

I don't answer. I can't. His fingers dip low, and the way he groans tells him everything.

"Gods…" he breathes. "You're dripping."

Then: "Let me taste what I've been dying to know."

And he does.

The first stroke of his tongue wrecks me. I cry out, arching as heat explodes low in my belly.

He groans—deep, guttural—like he didn't expect it to ruin him this much.

His arms wrap beneath my thighs as he pulls me to the edge of the bed, his mouth relentless, tongue stroking and curling and sucking in a rhythm that's devastating.

He's not careful. He's hungry.

I writhe beneath him, gasping, shaking, my fingers tangled in his hair like I need to anchor him there.

He groans again, deeper this time, the sound vibrating through my core. "You taste like you remember me," he moans into me.

And I do. Though it's my soul and not my body, my body reacts accordingly.

When I come, it's not soft—it's shattering. My thighs tremble. My voice breaks. I sob his name like it's the only word I've ever learned.

Still, he doesn't stop.

Not until I'm raw and twitching and completely undone beneath him.

Then he rises. Kisses his way up my stomach, my ribs, the curve of my breast, until he's hovering over me.

His hand strokes my jaw. Thumb brushes my lips. He lines himself up, thick and heavy and burning hot, dragging the tip through my wetness.

"This time," he growls, voice wrecked, "we finish what we started."

And then he pushes into me.

Slow. Deep. Stretching.

I gasp, mouth falling open as he fills me inch by inch—like he's carving his way into me. My back arches, and I cry out, gripping his shoulders as he bottoms out with a broken moan.

"Fuck, Jane…"

We move like we've done this before—somewhere, sometime, in a life we've barely remembered but never forgot.

His thrusts start slow and deep, hips rolling in waves that steal my breath.

He kisses me with every movement. Worships me with every drag of skin. Speaks with his body in a language older than blood.

Then he stills inside me. Deep. Still. Pressed.

His mouth finds my ear, breath hot and shaking.

"Say my name."

I can't breathe.

He thrusts once—hard, deep, devastating. "Say it when you come. So the whole world knows you're mine!"

And I do.

I fall apart around him with a cry, body clenching, vision blurred, soul burning.

"Alexander—" I scream, the sound ripped from my throat like a promise.

He groans into my neck, thrusts again, and comes with me—shuddering, gasping, whispering my name like a curse. Like a vow. Like salvation.

We collapse together.

Tangled in heat and stormlight, breathless and shaking, magic still thrumming faintly beneath our skin like an aftershock. The rain drums against the balcony rail. Candlelight flickers wildly. And somewhere beneath the bed, the grimoire pulses once, quiet and knowing.

His chest rises and falls against mine. One of his hands is in my hair, the other still clutching my hip like he can't quite let go.

And maybe he can't. Because I can't either.

In the silence that follows, trembling and slick with sweat and soul-deep exhaustion, I realize—

I don't know where he ends and I begin.

THE SPARK BENEATH THE STORM

We lie there in the quiet hum of candlelight and rain, tangled in each other like we've done this before—like our bodies remember. My head rests on his chest. I expect to find the steady rhythm of his heartbeat, but my own heart skips a beat when there is nothing to be heard. I take a deep breath, and for a while, I just breathe him in—cedar and storm and something faintly metallic, like old magic burned clean.

But the silence eventually gives way to questions.

I shift just enough to look up at him. His hand slides along my back absentmindedly, gentle and unhurried.

"Why now?" I ask softly. "Why haven't I heard from you since that night in the cemetery?"

He exhales through his nose, jaw tightening a little. "I was worried I'd been followed."

That wasn't the answer I expected.

"Followed? By who?"

He hesitates. Then, "There's a witch, a seer working with the rogue faction of vampires. Not someone sanctioned by the Council—this one's off-grid. Dangerous. My own seer contact caught wind of them sniffing around 'odd magic' here in New Orleans. That's their phrase.

Odd magic. It's not just any witch they're looking for. They're hunting someone strong enough to reopen the gate between realms."

My blood runs cold.

"And?" I press, already sensing there's more.

Alexander nods grimly. "There's something else. But we're not sure what. Both the rogue Vampire High Council's seer and my friend Morgaine…their visions are murky. Fragmented. Like something's deliberately shrouding the truth. Fogging the threads of magic."

I shiver and curl closer to him, then tell him everything—about the grimoire, the vision, the name Lyriën Velashara. About the prophecy. About my magic reacting before I ever meant it to. About the twin pull I feel inside me: one tethered to him and one I still don't fully understand.

He listens without interruption, his fingers moving in slow circles on my back.

Then he speaks.

"Vanessa and I…we discovered it together. Not just the prophecy. The truth behind it. That the souls we carried weren't just powerful— they were the originals. The first Eternal and the first witch. We didn't know what it meant. We tried to uncover more, to understand why we'd come back, but the war started. She was betrayed. Executed. And I barely escaped."

My throat tightens. "But if you fought for the witches and wolves, why weren't you marked to stay in this realm?"

He looks at me then, something haunted flickering in his eyes.

"I was marked," he says. "But the mark faded. A few weeks later, it was just gone. I've never heard of that happening to anyone else. I didn't say anything. I was afraid. If the Witches Council saw me as a threat, I knew I'd be hunted."

A lump forms in my throat.

"A couple years ago, I had a vision," he continues. "A girl born under a blood moon here in New Orleans. The same fire in her soul, the same storm in her magic. I came looking. Spent years gathering what I could. Watching. Researching reincarnation, trying to help Morgaine piece together her visions."

He brushes a damp strand of hair from my forehead.

"When I realized your birthday aligned with another blood moon… it was too big to ignore. Too much power converging at once. I knew you were the one. But I didn't mean to meet you in the cemetery that night. I just…I couldn't stay away anymore."

I hold his gaze, heart pounding. "I know our souls are tied. I know I've had flashes of memories that feel like they belonged to someone else, but I'm not her. I'm not Lyriën. I'm not Vanessa. I'm me."

I carry her soul, maybe even her fire, but my choices, my fears, my messy heart—that's all mine. I can't lose myself to a ghost, even if she lives inside me.

His smile is soft, warm, devastating.

He kisses my forehead.

"I know exactly who you are, Jane Agatha Fontenot," he whispers. "I've watched from a distance these last few years with nothing but admiration—for your kindness, your loyalty, your humor, your fire. You're brave in ways most people can't even name. Your laugh could light up the darkest night. You're not Vanessa. You're not Lyriën. You're you. Unapologetically, brilliantly you. Every curve, every thought, every tear. And when I look into your eyes, I see you. Only you."

I blink, and a tear slips free.

He catches it with his thumb.

"I can't tell you how hard it's been to stay away," he says. "But I wanted you to have some peace before everything started to unravel. And I didn't want to risk putting you in danger before I knew how I could help. I didn't realize you'd be able to feel me coming and going. I should've known."

Another tear falls, this one heavier.

He kisses it away, lips brushing my cheek like a promise.

Part of me wants to stay here forever—in this bed, in this warmth, in the comfort of his arms amid the storm outside. To disappear into the quiet hum of shared breath and soul-deep connection. Just a little longer.

But I know we can't.

We're close. So close to something bigger than either of us.

And I can feel it—just beneath the surface—rising like a tide.

"I want to stay here with you," I whisper. "Just for a while. But we're running out of time. We still don't know why our souls needed to come back. Why they keep finding each other. Who betrayed Vanessa. What the prophecy truly means. How we're connected to the Eternal Realm. And what the hell is going to happen to me under this blood moon…"

I glance at the flickering candles.

"…in just six days."

I don't get to finish the thought.

Because suddenly, he's shifting, flipping me gently beneath him with a low growl that vibrates against my skin. His mouth finds my throat, then my collarbone, then lower. Reverent. Hungry. Possessive.

"You don't even realize, do you?" he murmurs, voice like velvet over flame. "What you do to me. What you've always done."

His fangs slip down—not threatening, but aching with restraint. With need.

I shudder beneath him as his lips trail down my stomach, slow and worshipful.

His voice drops to something darker.

"We can go and do what we must, but before anything else, I want to taste you again, making you come until I hear my name melt off your lips."

Then he's between my thighs again, unhurried and devastating, tongue moving with practiced skill and deliberate intent. He takes his time, savoring each gasp and twitch like a man starving. His hands hold me steady, fingers gripping my hips as if I might vanish if he doesn't anchor me to this moment.

And then his fingers slide in. A slow stretch, then a perfect curl that has my head falling back with a cry. My thighs shake around him.

But he's not done.

He lifts one of my legs over his shoulder and nuzzles the inside of my thigh. Then…a kiss. Then the barest graze of fang against that tender skin.

A promise. A threat. A tease.

But he doesn't bite.

Instead, he pauses, watching me, eyes hooded with heat, lips parted, breath ragged.

I whimper, desperate and undone. I whisper breathlessly, "If you keep teasing me like that…"

He moves up my body, slow and hot and solid.

Then he lies back, arms sprawled across the pillows like a god offering himself to be worshiped. Or conquered.

"Then ride me," he says, his voice cracking open with want. "Show me how you burn."

I straddle him without hesitation, legs still trembling, heart hammering like thunder.

His hands find my waist, but they don't guide. They just hold, letting me lead. Letting me take. Letting me own this.

I sink onto him, slow and deep, and we both groan like we're breaking and fusing all at once. My nails dig into his chest. His head falls back against the pillow, jaw tight, every muscle in his body tensed like he's holding back an avalanche.

I start to move. Rolling. Grinding. Claiming.

It's not soft.

It's wild.

It's real.

And it's mine.

I brace my palms on his chest, riding him harder, faster—until heat floods my body and everything begins to blur. But then—

It happens.

My fingers begin to glow.

First just at the tips, like candlelight moving over my skin. Then brighter, until blue arcs of electricity crackle across my knuckles and pop down my arms. It doesn't hurt. It surges. A wild current, born from something ancient and buried and mine.

He sees it—eyes wide with awe and something close to reverence—but he doesn't stop me. He lets me burn.

My back arches, a cry tearing from my throat as my body shatters around him, and the magic bursts from my fingertips in a snap of electric light, searing the air with the scent of ozone and something older than language.

He groans beneath me, hands gripping my thighs, and we fall together—his name on my lips, mine on his, everything tangled in light and heat and the storm that lives in our skin.

And when it's over, I collapse against him, our bodies slick and breathless, my magic still humming like an aftershock.

Outside, thunder rumbles low.

Inside, I swear the candle flames lean toward us.

And in his arms, for one breathless moment, I'm not afraid of what I am.

Because for the first time, I know he sees me.

Only me.

And I've never felt more real.

Six days until the blood moon. The words coil in the back of my mind no matter how I try to ignore them. Every hour feels louder now, ticking toward something I don't understand yet.

SÉANCE
&
SUNDRY

CHAPTER ELEVEN

BLOODLINES AND BOUNDARIES

By the time the rain lets up, I already know what I need to do.

Alexander sits beside me, the stormlight softening the sharpness in his eyes. It's still strange, this quiet between us—both familiar and brand new. But there's no more room for hiding. Not from them. Not from myself.

I reach for my phone and type out the group message:

Me: *Need everyone at the shop in an hour. Family meeting. It's important.*

Fergus replies with a thumbs-up emoji. Braelynn, predictably, adds big eyes and fire emojis followed by, *"You okay?"* Javi just writes: *"Oooooh dramaaaa"* with a teacup. Maurice? No response yet. I stare at his name for a second longer than I mean to.

"You sure they're ready?" Alexander asks, his voice low, edged with that ancient weight he carries like a second skin.

"No," I admit. "But I'm not waiting anymore."

As I wait, I walk through Gran's private library in the back of the shop. It smells like dust and lavender, the kind of scent that seeps into the wood and never leaves. I've thumbed through these shelves a hundred times, but tonight something feels different—like the spines are watching me, waiting.

One of the oldest volumes sits crooked on the shelf, leather cracked and curling. Not the Velashara grimoire, but a family book, smaller, worn with use. The kind of thing passed down through hands that lived ordinary lives, not legendary ones.

When I pull it down, a slip of parchment flutters free, lodged deep between the pages. It isn't bound with the rest of the text, but hidden there on purpose. My pulse stutters as I ease it open.

The scroll is thin, almost fragile enough to dissolve in my hands. The ink has browned, but the words are sharp enough to sting:

"Seek the relic where the roots of Velashara broke stone. Within the tomb lies the fire and the blood, bound together until called."

A sketch runs along the edge—an old crypt, its arch marked with a crescent moon. Recognition twists in my chest. I've seen it before. Tucked away in St. Louis Cemetery No. 1. The Fontenot tomb. My family's tomb.

The air in the library shifts, cooler now, pressing in against my skin. I fold the scroll carefully, but it feels less like discovery and more like awakening—as if the book had been waiting for me all along. I fill Gran in quickly, and by the time she has a chance to look over everything, everyone starts to arrive.

The bell above the door chimes just before ten.

Javi breezes in first, swirling his cloak dramatically like he's on a stage none of us paid for. "Darlings," he sings, "I bring gossip and gifts. Both are me. You're welcome."

Fergus and B follow close behind. She's got that look—suspicious curiosity wrapped in a leather jacket and barely restrained growl. Fergus offers me a gentle nod, but his eyes flick to Alexander and stay there, narrowed.

"Everyone grab a seat," I say, nerves skittering like static under my skin. "There's…a lot."

Javi's eyes land on Alexander and go wide. "Ohhhhh." He leans toward B and stage-whispers, "Is this the reason she's been glowing like someone lit a candle under her sheets?"

"Javi." I pinch the bridge of my nose, but a corner of my mouth threatens to betray me with a smile.

Then the front door swings open again.

Maurice.

He stops dead in the doorway, scanning the room. His gaze lands on Alexander and freezes. One heartbeat. Two. Then his jaw clenches.

"Who the fuck is this?"

Alexander stands slowly, elegant and measured, like a king who's seen a thousand battles and still chooses grace. "Alexander. And you must be Maurice."

"Oh, I must, huh?" Maurice steps closer, posture rigid. "Funny how you know who I am when she's said jack shit about you."

"Maurice," I warn, stepping between them. "Stop."

"No, J." He looks down at me, betrayal barely masked by the flicker of something deeper. "You've been through hell, and now suddenly there's some vampire playing bodyguard? You don't think we deserve a heads-up?"

Alexander doesn't flinch. "I'm not just a bodyguard."

"Clearly. I can smell it all over you both."

Javi fans himself from the corner. "Is it hot in here, or is that just the alpha posturing? I live for a showdown."

Maurice doesn't budge.

His arms stay locked across his chest, jaw working like he's chewing back a growl.

Braelynn lets out a slow, pointed sigh. "Damn, Mo. Want to punch a wall while you're at it?"

He doesn't respond. Just stares straight ahead like Alexander's presence alone is a challenge.

She steps a little closer to both of us, but keeps her voice even. "Look, we're all surprised. And yeah, the vampire thing's a twist." Her eyes flick to Alexander, then back to Maurice. "But if Jane says she's safe, then she's safe. So maybe chill with the brooding 'mine' energy and take a fucking seat."

Maurice's lip curls. "You think I'm being dramatic?"

"I know you're being dramatic," she snaps back, but there's a flicker of concern in her eyes. "You're not usually this much of an ass unless something actually matters."

That lands heavier than it should.

I glance at Alexander, who says nothing, but I feel his hand tighten ever so slightly around mine. Seeing them together is like standing between fire and lightning—both dangerous, both familiar, both pulling at me in ways I don't understand. Maurice feels like home, steady and grounding. Alexander feels like a storm I've already drowned in once before. And I don't know why being near them at the same time makes my chest ache, like I'll split apart if I choose and shatter if I don't.

I tell myself it's just circumstance, just the blood moon stirring up things I can't explain. But when Maurice's gaze catches mine and Alexander's shadow brushes against me in the same breath, I can't deny it anymore—something in me belongs to both, and I hate how much it tears me open.

We don't even make it to the back before the scent of rosemary and melted wax meets us. When we step down into the reading room of Séance & Sundry, Gran is already waiting—seated with a cup of tea, calm as ever, but her eyes flicker sharply when she sees Alexander.

She sets her mug down slowly. "Well. You must be the guest Jane mentioned."

Alexander gives a small bow, voice smooth but reverent. "I am. It's an honor to meet you, ma'am."

Gran studies him with quiet intensity, but her tone stays even. "You're older than you look."

He nods. "That tends to happen."

There's a pause before he adds, "Jane is remarkable. Stronger than most I've known and still kind. I imagine that's because of you."

Gran's expression softens slightly, something proud and weathered behind her eyes. "She came into this world in fire and loss. But she's always had light in her."

Alexander meets her gaze. "She still does. And I'm grateful she had someone who saw it."

Gran doesn't smile, but she doesn't argue either. "Then let's see if we can keep it lit."

The next hour passes in a current of updates and unraveling truths.

We fill everyone in—everything Alexander and I now know, everything the grimoire has whispered, everything the prophecy has started to reveal. The name. The verse. The blood moon. The mark that no longer protects him. The rogue seer tracking "odd magic."

When we review the questions and gaps still looming in the next six days, the list feels heavier than ever:

- Why hasn't the grimoire opened for me?
- Who—and what—was the original Eternal?
- What happens if the gate opens on the blood moon?
- What exactly are the rogue vampires trying to bring through?

Braelynn taps her fingers against the side of her chair, restless. "You know, I've been in this world my whole damn life, and this still feels bigger than any of us. Like we're playing catch-up in a game no one told us we were in."

Gran nods slowly. "That's exactly what it is."

B shrugs, eyes flicking to me. "Then we better learn the rules fast. Or write our own."

Javi perches on the arm of Gran's chair, twirling one of his rings. "Also—just so we're stacking our stress neatly—I've heard something from one of my not-so-loyal Council contacts."

We all turn.

"There's talk," he continues, "that the gate's magic, the seal is weakening. Naturally. The Council thinks it'll fully start to waver within the next year. Maybe sooner. And if the vampires figure that out first—and they will, because they have a seer now—they might not need to wait for the veil to thin on its own."

Fergus frowns. "So if the gate's already thinning…"

"They wouldn't need a full moon, just someone strong enough to break it open. And they'd want to kill anyone who threatens to seal it," Javi finishes.

"And they've got a seer," Braelynn adds. "Which means they're planning something. Actively."

"Exactly," I say quietly. "We're behind. They're already plotting. Already sniffing around the Quarter. And if they figure out how to force the gate before the veil lifts naturally…"

"We won't be ready," Gran finishes. "And we can't call on other covens or packs until we know more. It has to be sanctioned by the Council—and by your father, B."

B lets out a sharp breath, eyes narrowing. *"Of course it comes back to him,"* she mutters, jaw tight.

Gran's voice is steady, but her eyes betray the weight behind her words. "If they open the gate, or the seal fails, it won't just be the banished vampires crawling back through. They'll come in force, and with them, things we've only heard whispers of. Creatures that were never meant to walk this world."

She clears her throat.

"Jane found something," she says, pulling a folded scrap of parchment. "It was tucked behind a spellbinding page in our old family grimoire, like it was meant to stay hidden until someone needed it."

She looks up at me, her green eyes sharp. "There's a passage about an old family tomb. One of the original Fontenot settlers—buried in Cemetery One. It says the tomb was sealed with blood magic to protect a relic passed down through the Velashara line."

My heart skips. "What kind of relic?"

Gran hesitates. "It doesn't say exactly. Just that it once belonged to Lyriën Velashara herself. And that it's bound with blood magic—it won't awaken unless the one it's meant for stands before it."

I swallow hard, already knowing what she was about to say.

"I think it's you, Jane." Her voice softens. "I think you're the one it's been waiting for. That's why you were drawn to it."

She places the parchment gently on the table.

"We don't have much else to go on right now," she continues. "And time's running out. Whatever's coming…I think that relic might be the key to surviving it." The silence that follows feels like the moment before a match is struck.

After the group starts to disperse, I step into the hallway just off the reading room with Gran beside me. The air feels heavier out here—quieter, too.

She looks at me like she's seeing more than I'm saying. "He's important to you," she says gently.

I nod. "And somehow…always has been."

Gran reaches out and tucks a curl behind my ear. "Then trust that. But don't let one soul bond blind you to your own path. You've always been more than just someone's legacy."

I swallow, blinking hard. "I know. I just didn't expect Maurice to take it so hard."

"You didn't expect it to affect you as much either."

I don't answer. I don't need to.

In the main room, Maurice is already at the door. Alexander moves to speak, but Maurice beats him to it.

"You say you love her?" Maurice asks, his voice low but sharp.

Alexander doesn't waver. "I do."

I freeze. My mouth goes dry hearing his declaration. We've only just met—at least, I have. My soul may remember him, may burn with centuries of knowing, but my heart and my head don't. Not yet. To me, he's still a stranger with eyes like a storm, claiming pieces of me I don't understand. Part of me wants to lean into it, into him, because the weight of that love feels like gravity itself. But the other part of me fights back, reminding me that I'm Jane, not Vanessa, not Lyriën. I'm not ready to hand myself over to a history I don't remember living. His love feels fated, yes—but it also feels like a trap, one I'm not sure I can survive.

Maurice nods once. Then takes a step closer, eyes locking with his. "Then don't give me a reason not to believe you."

Alexander holds his gaze. "I won't."

Maurice gives a humorless half-smile, almost like a warning.

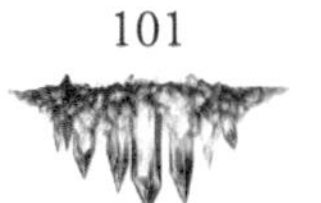

Then he turns without another word and pulls the shop door open.

The bell above it rings, sharp and final. And then he's gone.

Five days. That's all the space between me and whatever waits beneath that red sky—yet all I can feel is the hollow he left behind, as if when Maurice walked out the door, he took the air with him.

CHAPTER TWELVE

THE TOMB AND TRUTH

Braelynn walks ahead with purpose, Fergus close behind her. Javi had stayed behind at Séance & Sundry, digging through family grimoires and old coven records—searching for anything on the Velashara lineage, on lightning sigils, or how to unlock a sealed grimoire that refuses to speak.

"We'll circle back by the time the sun's down," B said, squeezing my arm before she and Fergus disappeared down the levee path. "You'll be fine."

Gran walks a few paces ahead now, humming softly to herself—a spell of protection, or maybe memory. The folded parchment she found in our old family grimoire is tucked securely into her bag, and I can feel its weight like a second heartbeat.

We pass through the Quarter's quieter edge, where the noise thins and the streets begin to settle into shadow. The iron gate to Cemetery One looms ahead, half-draped in ivy, the names on its outer arch faded.

The air shifts the moment we step through the cemetery gates.

Everything stills.

The scent of old stone and magnolia hangs thick in the silence, and even the breeze feels reverent, like it knows not to speak too loudly here. Gran doesn't pause. She moves with purpose, the soft swish of her shawl brushing against the cracked path as she leads us deeper into the rows of tombs.

I slow for just a second, dragging in a breath.

Then I hear it.

Footsteps behind me. Familiar. Measured.

I turn, and my heart stumbles.

Maurice.

He steps into view from the narrowing corridor between tombs, hands in the pockets of his jacket, his expression unreadable beneath the overcast sky.

"I thought you took off," I say, voice lower than I expect.

He shrugs, gaze flicking over the cemetery before settling on me. "I couldn't just sit around wondering."

I blink, stunned—but not unhappy to see him.

Gran glances back briefly but says nothing, nodding once before continuing.

Maurice falls into step beside me. Closer than I expected.

Too close, maybe.

His arm brushes mine, just barely. But it's enough.

Enough to make my pulse stutter, my breath catch. The warmth of him lingers long after the contact ends, curling down my spine like something remembered.

And then I catch it.

His scent.

It's not the same as before. Not quite.

Still Maurice—still warmth and cedar and late autumn—but something underneath has shifted. Wilder. Sharper. Like the edge of a storm hiding behind a clear sky. Like something old stirring awake beneath his skin.

I inhale again, quieter this time, not sure if I'm imagining it.

It hits deeper this time. Like static in my lungs.

It shouldn't affect me the way it does. Not this much. But it coils through my senses like recognition and lightning and something I don't have a name for.

He must feel it too because he glances at me.

And for one long, quiet second, we just hold each other's gaze.

No words. Just that flicker of something barely restrained between us. Old longing. New tension. A question neither of us is brave enough to ask.

I break the gaze first, clearing my throat and looking straight ahead. He doesn't move away.

We walk together in silence, the tombs rising like watchful sentries around us as the city fades behind.

And ahead—waiting in quiet stone and shadow—is the truth.

Rows of tombs stretch before us in crumbling elegance, marble stained with moss and time. Even in a city steeped in death, Cemetery One carries a weight of its own.

Gran leads the way, a folded map clutched tight in her hand, her shawl fluttering like a banner in the humid breeze.

"This way," she murmurs, her voice low but certain. "The Fontenot crypt is toward the back. Most people think it's empty. The name worn off the stone was intentional. A shield. The real story's been buried for centuries."

Maurice walks beside me, his steps slower now, more measured. His presence is quiet but steady, like he's trying not to disturb something sacred.

"You sure you want to be here?" I ask softly.

He glances at me. "I told you. I'm not leaving you alone in this."

We don't speak again as we follow Gran through the narrow stone paths, the hush of the cemetery pressing in around us like fog. Somewhere nearby, a bird calls once, then goes silent.

Finally, we stop.

The tomb is plain: weathered stone, cracked nameplate. Ivy climbs the sides like fingers trying to pull it back into the earth.

"This is it," Gran says, crouching by the sealed iron gate around the tomb. "It belonged to Jean Fontenot, one of the founding settlers and one of our blood. But the records were erased. Quietly. The relic inside…it's older than this land. It belonged to Lyriën herself."

My breath catches.

Gran presses her palm to the lock. "It's bound by blood magic. It'll only open for the one it's meant for."

She steps back. Looks at me.

I nod. Then step forward.

The moment my fingers brush the cold metal, something flares beneath my skin—heat and static and memory all at once.

A click.

Then the gate groans open. Followed by the sound of stone sliding. A doorway into the Tomb appears—it wasn't there before.

The air inside the tomb is cooler, but not stale. It smells of stone, candlewax, and something older. Something electric.

We descend into a single chamber beneath the tomb. It's small, but clean. Preserved. As if time itself were warded away.

At the center, atop a black stone pedestal, rests a circular relic.

It's obsidian-smooth, marked with lightning-like etchings that pulse faintly in the dim light. Next to it, a scroll sealed in red wax waits, its sigil unfamiliar but somehow intimate.

Gran steps forward slowly, reverently. "This isn't Council magic," she whispers. "It's ours. Pure Velashara. Before the hiding."

I reach out. The scroll cracks open at my touch.

"To the one who bears the blood and the soul, this message will find you. The rest must wait."

My eyes drift to the relic.

It calls to me.

I place my hand on it.

A spark. Then—

The world falls away.

Light explodes behind my eyes. Not white, not gold—something older. A burnished silver-blue, like moonlight filtered through memory. I'm no longer standing in the tomb.

I'm somewhere else.

A field of stars.

And she's there.

She stands barefoot in the stillness, hair loose around her shoulders like a silver river kissed by flame. Her eyes are green—like mine—but older. Wiser. Brimming with sorrow and fire. She looks at me with a kind of aching recognition.

"My name is Lyriën," she says. Her voice doesn't echo in my ears—it echoes through me.

She steps closer, and though I don't move, the space between us folds in on itself.

"I was the first," she says. "The beginning. The bloodline that bore your name before it was ever spoken aloud. If you're seeing this, a piece of me is within you."

Images flicker across her features—her memories, not mine. A man with silver-gold eyes. A touch that made the air tremble. A kiss that defied death.

"His name was Thaedryn," she says, and I feel the weight of it—the name I didn't know I was waiting for. "He was the Eternal. The one who loved me beyond this life. He died first, holding me in his arms after a battle that should've taken us both. I followed him soon after."

Her voice grows quieter. Heavier.

"His soul did not fade. It could not. It was bound by fate to return—reborn in a human vessel that would one day be turned vampire. A cruel irony. A necessary balance. Even though he walks now as what the world calls an enemy, he is still part of us. Still part of you."

I see him then—Alexander. His face flickers between what it is now and what it once was. Thaedryn's eyes, softened by pain and lifetimes lost.

"There is a reason the bond between you is so strong," Lyriën continues. "You are both soul keepers. Two halves. Bound by magic and time. The Eternal Return."

She lifts her hand, and stars shimmer between her fingers.

"We had a daughter. She carried both the fire in her blood and the light from the sky. But before I died, I saw a vision of a flame rekindled. A moon reborn. A child of the bloodline who would awaken our legacy when the world needed us again."

The vision shifts.

I see myself—again and again—across centuries. A hundred lives I don't remember but somehow know. I see Thaedryn's soul woven through each one, always circling mine. Sometimes missing. Sometimes near.

"The grimoire you found…and this tomb," Lyriën says, her voice pulled thin by time. "They were placed here when our bloodline crossed the sea. When this city was still being carved from swamp and stone. We blended into the bayou's oldest magic, knowing one day, the line would return. New Orleans is not just a crossroads of culture. It is a convergence of realms. The city breathes magic into the bones of those who carry it. That is why your power stirs here. That is why the vault opened only for you."

She steps closer, her presence warmer now.

"But your bloodline…it is not just your soul that holds power. You were born of me. And your father—his birth marked the first break in the line of women since I first walked this world. That break was meant to happen. If my vision was correct, all will reveal itself beneath the blood moon."

The stars behind her burn brighter. And then the world shifts again.

Fire. Screams. Red eyes flashing in darkened streets. Shadows crawling across cities. Smoke rising where people once stood.

"Vampires were never meant for this realm," she says, voice iron now. "They came through the gate long ago—uninvited. And if they remain, they will consume everything. Not because they are evil, but because their nature demands it. This world was not made to hold them."

She lifts her hand.

Two shadowed figures appear at the edge of a cliff, bathed in silver light. Behind them, a glowing rift pulses like a second moon. The gate between realms.

"There is only one way to close the gate. Permanently. It must be done by the combined force of both soul keepers. You and him."

I can feel the pressure of it all coiling inside me. The weight. The inevitability.

But Lyriën's gaze softens again.

"I cannot tell you more," she says. "The magic will show you. The moment will come."

The air stills around us. Her voice dips lower.

"You must be careful. Pressing too hard against what has not yet ripened can break the threads that bind this path. Every choice you make shapes the next. Every truth must come at its time or risk unraveling everything we've worked to protect."

A pause. Then: "Do not rush fate. Let it arrive in its rhythm. That is the only way the ending can hold."

The light dims. I smell the scent of moss and stone beginning to return.

She steps forward one last time and places a hand gently to my cheek. Her touch is warm. Familiar. Like my grandmother's. Like memory.

"I'm sorry this falls upon your shoulders, sweet girl," she whispers. "You are stronger than you'll ever know. And even though fragments of me are within you, you are still very much yourself. Don't ever forget that."

Behind her, the grimoire hovers, still closed but glowing faintly.

"It will open," she says, backing into the fading starlight. "When it's time."

And just like that—

The vision breaks.

GOOD ENOUGH TO BURN

The days between the tomb and the blood moon pass in fragments. The days slipped by faster than I could hold them. One heartbeat, it was four days left, and now the blood moon is a breath away.

I sleep too much or not at all. Eat only when B or Gran places something in front of me. The rest of the time, I drift through the hours like a phantom—half in this world, half somewhere else entirely.

There's too much I still don't understand. Too many pieces of this puzzle that feel just out of reach, like they're hovering behind frosted glass. The tomb gave me truths, yes—but not all of them. I can feel that. Like there's something else just beyond the veil of what I've been shown, something I need before all of this truly makes sense.

Alexander hasn't come by since the night after I saw Lyriën.

He did show up. Quietly. Candlelight and shadows curled behind him as he stood on my balcony like he always does. I almost didn't let him in because I knew what would happen if I did.

But I did. And when I saw the look in his eyes—soft, searching, with that faint tilt of worry I pretended not to understand—I told him the truth.

"I can't think clearly when you're near me," I said.

He didn't argue. Just stepped back, gave a shallow nod, and vanished into the storm without another word.

So now there's just…space. The kind that feels like both a gift and a curse. I haven't decided yet if him giving me space makes him respectful or just scared. Maybe it's both. Maybe he's waiting for me to figure myself out first. Or maybe he's not sure he's allowed to want me in the middle of all this.

And honestly? I'm not sure either.

But I can still feel him, like static just outside the edge of awareness. Like he's still watching. Still waiting. Letting me breathe. Letting me decide.

Fergus, on the other hand, has been all movement and muscle and muttered swear words. He's been doubling down on patrols with Kaia, running interference around the Quarter, and making sure the younger wolves steer clear of trouble. "If this blood moon's gonna blow the lid off things," he said, dragging a clawed hand through his curls, "I'd rather not be babysitting a bunch of hormonal pups while it happens." B says he hasn't slept more than three hours in a row since the rogue sightings started. Not that he'd admit it.

And Javi?

Javi's been diving into dusty archives like a glam archaeologist on a mission. He's been hopping between Séance & Sundry and the coven's restricted stacks, cross-referencing sigils, lineage scrolls, and Council whispers. He hasn't told me much, only that he's "getting close to something weird" and that the High Council's energy has been unusually reactive. He takes the lead with council snooping because otherwise it could catch too much attention if it were Gran. Though she still leads the coven here, her involvement with the council has been few and far between these last years. She has never been much for politics, and she felt it was safer for me as things began to shift. Poor Javi's eyeliner has been more warpaint than glam lately, and even his snark has been quieter. Which is probably the most terrifying development of all.

Everyone's preparing in their own way.

And me? I'm just trying not to spiral. When the walls start closing in, I scrub counters until they shine or rearrange shelves in the shop like order on the outside might quiet the chaos inside. I'll sweep the same corner three times, polish brass until my hands ache, anything to keep moving. Because if I stop—if I sit still long enough—the tide of it all threatens to drag me under.

The more the blood moon creeps closer, the more I feel like I'm walking a tightrope over something vast and burning. My skin hums with nerves. My thoughts scatter in too many directions, looping and replaying conversations and warnings and symbols until I can't tell what's helpful and what's just noise.

My anxiety—already a high-functioning nightmare—can't handle any more anticipation. Not when I'm carrying so much and expected to make sense of it like I don't process the world like a damn motherboard flooded with static. I need something to happen. Anything. Because if I have to sit in this limbo of knowing-not-knowing any longer, I might unravel entirely.

My anxiety spirals through the same five thoughts like a carousel I can't get off, and no amount of tea, pacing, or distraction is enough to quiet the feeling that something's coming. That something is already here. Tomorrow night is the night, but tonight the gang wants to have a fun night out for my birthday. It's not typically my style, but tonight, I needed out.

Out of my head. Out of the house. Out of the ache I keep pretending isn't sitting just beneath my skin. B had texted twice and then threatened to send Fergus upstairs with glitter in his *hair* if I didn't answer.

So here I was, eyeliner sharp, mouth glossed, and wearing a black skirt that flirts with my thighs when I walked. I haven't worn it in ages. It makes me feel like someone who still knew how to take up space.

"You look hot," B says the second I step out. "Like, 'don't touch her unless you've got a death wish' hot."

"She always looks hot," Javi adds, sipping something pink and overly dramatic. "And I didn't bring the glitter. *This time.*"

Fergus gives a bashful smile. "Jane, you look really nice."

I smile—real and slow. It feels good.

Until I see Maurice.

Leaning against the porch railing, arms crossed, T-shirt stretched across his chest in a way that should be illegal. He looks me up and down once—just once—and the flicker in his eyes makes my stomach lurch. His jaw tightens.

Not a word. Just that slow, deliberate smirk. Like he knows exactly what he was doing to me. I feel trickles of anxiety creep up my spine.

The bar on Frenchmen is packed, pulsing with brass and heat and life. The kind of place where the music vibrated through your ribs and made you forget everything else.

We find a corner booth just off the dance floor. B drags Fergus into the fray before he could object, and to all of our surprise, he thrives. The man could move.

"I love this for him," I whisper to Javi.

"He's officially hotter than all of us," he replies. "My self-worth is in shambles."

Javi stands and heads to the dance floor to join them. "You coming?" he says. I smile. "Yeah, I'll come out here soon. Waiting to hear my jam!"

I'm on my second drink—something citrusy and slightly dangerous—when I feel Maurice slide into the seat beside me.

He doesn't say anything at first. Just sits close enough that our thighs brush. Just enough to make me feel like every molecule in my body has suddenly decided to wake up.

"You always wear jeans," he says eventually, voice low.

I don't look at him. "You keeping notes?"

"Apparently."

I take a slow sip, trying to play it cool.

"You look…" He trails off.

I finally turn to meet his eyes. "Yeah?"

"Like I should get on my knees and thank the moon you were born."

My heart stumbles. I laugh, but it cracks at the edges. "That's dramatic, even for you."

His voice dips closer to my ear. "You look good enough to eat, Jane."

Oh. Shit.

My breath catches. A flush crawls up my chest. My thighs press together under the table, and I hate—*hate*—how much I want him to follow through.

To distract myself, I looked out across the bar.

B is mid-spin, her wild curls catching air as she throws her head back and laughs. Kaia had shown up not long after the first round, all black boots and icy blonde confidence, sliding in like she was been summoned. She doesn't hesitate—just grabs B by the hand and pulls her into the dance with that cocky little smirk that says *I dare you not to have fun with me.*

They are magnetic together, glowing in their own strange orbit.

Javi and Fergus joined them, doing some kind of ridiculous duo routine that looked half-dance, half-drunken pantomime. Javi is singing along dramatically, Fergus is laughing so hard he can barely stand upright, and I catch myself grinning like a fool into my drink.

Even Gran is clapping from her spot in the back corner, her rings catching the light as she bops in her seat. Her smile is soft, proud. I can almost hear her thoughts: *This is what we're meant to protect.*

And gods, it is beautiful—this messy, magical little group we'd all somehow cobbled together.

I watch them like I'm watching a memory being made. One I wante to press between the pages of my life like a flower. Fragile, fleeting, but real.

"You look like you're memorizing it."

His voice slides in softly beside me, familiar and deep.

"Maybe I am," I say eventually. "Feels like one of those nights you'll want to remember. Before the world shifts again."

He nodded slowly, and for a second we just sit there in the thick of the music and laughter and flickering light.

Then he turns, his gaze catching mine with a steadiness that made my breath pause halfway in my chest.

"Come dance with me."

Not a command. Not a tease.

An offering.

And in that moment, I forget how to say no.

He leads me onto the floor with a hand at my back, light but grounding. The music wraps around us—slow enough to sway, soft enough to pretend we weren't burning. I feels the warmth of his palm as it slides to my waist, the way his other hand gently captures mine. And when our eyes meet again, something in him shifted.

I don't remember the song, just the way the beat matched the rhythm of my pulse.

Maurice pulls me in close. One hand at my waist. The other wrapped around my wrist like he wasn't quite ready to let go.

His body against mine is unfair. Solid. Warm. Familiar in a way that made my throat tighten.

We move in sync—too close for casual. Too slow for friendly. And when I shift my weight, my thigh brushes between his legs, and I feel the way his breath hitched.

He leans in again, mouth near my ear.

"I'm trying so hard not to touch you the way I want to."

My knees nearly buckles.

I don't respond. I can't. If I did, I'd unravel right here on the dance floor.

So I just kept dancing. One hand on his chest. One thought in my head:

Don't fall.

I step away eventually, needing space, needing air. My skirt sways as I make my way to the bar, bare legs catching cool air, heart still pounding.

I lean against the bar, waiting for my drink and trying to convince myself that stepping away for air was about the crowd, not about him. Maurice. Of course it has to be him tonight, suddenly deciding to turn up the charm after years of careful distance. My chest still aches from the way I brushed him off, regret crawling in before the glass even hits the counter. Why now? Why me? Why does he get to look at me like that—like I've always been his—when I can barely look at him without my pulse skipping like it's late for something?

And then someone grabs me.

A stranger's hand wraps tight around my wrist.

Too tight.

Something primal surges up my spine.

I don't think—*I* move. Twisted. Stepped in. Pinned his wrist against my body and shoved him off with a sharp pivot.

The man stumbles back, cursing. Rage lines his eyes, his body shifting to come towards me.

Before I can blink, Maurice is there.

He doesn't walk—he appears.

He shoves the guy back with one hand, teeth bared. "Touch her again," he growls, "and I'll break more than your hand."

The man, drunk and stupid, reaches again.

Crack.

The snap of bone is immediate and clean. The guy screams, falling to the floor, clutching his arm.

Maurice doesn't even flinch. He is still standing between me and the man, breathing heavy, eyes wild.

I touch his arm. "Maurice—"

He turns toward me.

"You shouldn't have to protect yourself," he says, voice tight. "Not when I'm here."

We left fast after that. No questions. No apologies. B told me Gran left before the chaos. The others were quiet, trailing a few feet behind as we walked through the Quarter.

Maurice walks beside me.

Close.

Silent.

And burning.

The night air cools my skin, but it doesn't matter. I can still feel him. The ghost of his hand on my back. The heat of his breath against my ear.

My body is humming. Every step we take is a scream inside my chest.

I steal a glance at him. His jaw is tight. Hands are in his pockets like he is trying not to reach for me.

I swallow hard. My skirt flutters around my legs with every step, like it remembers the way he looked at me when I walked away earlier.

God, Jane. Get a grip.

But I can't stop wondering. If I turn to him now, just a little, would he kiss me?

Would I let him?

Would I stop him?

I pull my arms in closer, forcing space between us. Just enough to breathe. I am such a lightweight, I can't believe I am acting this way. *Jesus, Jane. Get it together.* But in all honesty, if he touched me again tonight, I'm not sure I'll come back from it.

And maybe I didn't want to.

CHAPTER FOURTEEN

THE SHAPE OF SECRETS

We've decided to gather—pack and coven alike—armed and prepared as best we can for whatever happens beneath the blood moon. The clearing is thick with magic.

Lanterns swing gently from the moss-draped branches, casting flickering halos of light across the circle. The full blood moon hangs low in the sky, swollen and crimson, bleeding light into every shadow.

Pack and coven have gathered, not as a frequent habit, but as they once did when the original pact was first formed. Over the years, they've only come together like this on rare nights of great importance. Tonight is one of those nights.

Javi stands on one side of the circle, jaw tight, fingers twitching with barely concealed energy. B is across from him, eyes sharp, body wound tight like a spring. Kaia and Fergus flank the outer edges, their gazes scanning the trees like sentinels.

I stand at the edge of the circle, heart thudding hard, breath shallow. My usual clothes cling to my skin with the humidity and weight of anticipation. My palms won't stop tingling.

Gran is nearby, a small smile of reassurance pressed into her lips, though I can tell she's bracing for something. We all are.

And there, half-concealed in the tree line, is Alexander.

He doesn't step forward. Doesn't interfere. Just watches. The glow of the blood moon paints his skin silver and red, his expression un-

readable—but I feel him. A quiet anchor, letting me breathe, letting me choose.

Something shifts. Not outside—*in* me. The air grows heavier, like it is holding its breath. My skin tingles, like the edge of a spark trying to catch. I inhale, but it doesn't feel like enough. Something inside me stirs, low and electric, and I freeze mid-sentence.

Maurice's voice breaks through the haze, quiet but clear as he stands next to me. "Hey. You okay?"

I turn to him. His eyes are already on me—sharp, attentive, like he'd felt it too.

"Yeah," I say, though my voice sounds thinner than I mean it to. "Just a weird moment. Like the air shifted."

His brow furrows, but not with worry—more like recognition. "It did. Around you."

I look down, suddenly unsure. "Probably just nerves. Or low blood sugar."

But when I glance up again, he is still watching me. Not like I am about to break—but like something in me has just changed.

Then—

A surge of heat roars through my spine. My vision floods with white. Lightning cracks and flashes in the sky, and the lanterns flare the moment my breath caught. Not brighter… just alive. As if the fire has been waiting for me to remember it.

The ground tilts, and I gasp—not in pain, but in release.

I feel it before I see it—my body pulling apart and coming back together, reshaped. Bone cracking. Skin glowing. Not tearing, but shifting, like truth finally unfurling. The breath caught in my throat like it was trying to become something else.

It starts in my spine—an ache deep and molten that stretches outward in a slow, burning crawl. My knees buckle. I gasp, but the sound comes out strangled, foreign. The ground sways beneath me, or maybe I was swaying. I couldn't tell.

Then everything breaks open.

I try to scream, but it comes out a howl. My vision blurs, colors smearing into gold and shadow. The world tilts.

No—I'm here, I'm here, I'm—

—not.

My thoughts shatter into something raw, wordless. Fire blooms in my blood. Lightning arcs down my spine. Every heartbeat roars like wind through trees. And beneath it all, something ancient and wild rises to meet me.

When I land, I am on four legs. My paws hit the forest floor with a muted thud, grounding me in a reality that feels both entirely foreign and achingly right. The cool earth beneath them sends a jolt of recognition through me, like I've touched something I was always meant to return to.

The world sharpens. Every sound, every scent, every flicker of wind against fur becomes thunder in my ears.

Gasps ripple through the crowd.

I am a wolf.

Not just any wolf.

White as snow, with a single black streak down my back like lightning split my soul in two.

And across the circle, staring at me wide-eyed, is Braelynn.

She's shifted too.

The same white coat. The same black streak.

Her eyes meet mine—and in that moment, neither of us speaks, but something ancient and familiar clicks. Recognition. Not yet understanding. But something undeniable. That's not possible.

My mind scrambles for reason, for logic, for anything to explain how the girl who'd been my best friend since childhood is now staring at me like a mirror with breath and bone.

And in that moment, something inside me shifts.

Not just the fur or the form. Not even the magic. Deeper than all of that. A tether pulling tight. A blood-deep recognition.

Not just friend. Not just pack.

The thought slams into me with no mercy, no softness.

Then—

Maurice.

He is frozen, his eyes wide, unblinking, as I meet his gaze through a wolf's eyes. In that suspended second, I see him—his awe, his shock, the way something in his chest cracks open.

Then his voice breaks like a prayer as he drops to his knees before me. "My mate."

The words are reverent. Unbelieving. True.

The words land like thunder.

A few heads turn.

Braelynn catches the moment. Her eyes widen.

And just as the bond clicks into place, something flashes between us—not memory, not dream—something shared.

In a flash—

We see it.

A shared vision.

Us—running side by side, human, laughing through moonlit woods. Then—without hesitation—we shift, together, our bodies snapping into wildness mid-stride, white and golden brown blurs vanishing beneath the trees.

The moment stretches. Then, I break it. I bolt.

Not from fear. From being overwhelmed.

From the fact that everything is happening too fast, and yet too late.

I don't remember running.

Only flashes—branches tearing past me, moonlight rippling through the trees, my own heartbeat thudding like war drums in my chest. I ran until my legs couldn't carry the storm anymore.

Now I'm here. Back at the shop.

The familiar creak of the back door welcomes me, still half-open from earlier. I step inside on silent paws, the scent of beeswax, sage, and cinnamon settling around me like a memory. It's quiet—just the soft pop of the fire in the back hearth.

Gran is sitting in her armchair with a bowl of gumbo balanced in her lap, spoon paused midair.

She doesn't scream. Doesn't flinch.

Just sets the bowl down and rises slowly, eyes shining behind her spectacles.

"Oh, my sweet Janey," she whispers, stepping forward.

I whine—low and broken—unsure if it's a greeting or an apology. My legs tremble beneath me. I haven't shifted back. I can't. I don't even know how.

But she doesn't wait.

She kneels, wraps her arms around my trembling body, and strokes the space between my ears like she used to when I was small and scared of thunderstorms.

"I don't know how this is possible," she murmurs. "Not truly. Not unless…"

Her hand stills.

"Unless it's the Eternal's magic in your blood. That's the only explanation I have. The wolf bite your mother took while she was pregnant—that's what triggered the early labor, what killed her. The venom must have reached you in the womb. But even then, supernatural bloodlines have never merged like this. Not in any of our histories."

She pulls back just enough to look into my eyes. Her hand gently cups the side of my muzzle.

"But we'll figure it out, my sweet. We always do."

I lower myself slowly, folding into the rug at her feet, the fire casting flickers of gold across the floor. My wolf body presses into her lap. I let out a soft sigh—more breath than sound—and rest my head against her.

She hums. Not a spell this time, but something older. A lullaby she used to sing when I was teething and too restless to sleep.

The storm still rages outside, but here—curled against her, the scent of her herb-stained fingers grounding me—I feel safe.

I don't need answers tonight. I just need this.

CHAPTER FIFTEEN

BETWEEN MOUTH AND MEMORY

I wake with the taste of ash in my mouth and the scent of rain still clinging to my skin.

The sheets are tangled around my legs, damp with sweat—or maybe memory. My body aches, but not the way it does after nightmares. This is deeper. Like I've been remade and my bones haven't caught up yet.

Sunlight spills across the hardwood floor, casting everything in that too-honest golden hue of the morning after. My bedroom is still. Quiet. Nothing out of place. Except me.

I don't remember how I got here.

The last thing I remember is the firelight and Gran's arms. The warmth of her lap, the way her fingers moved over my fur like a lullaby. I must've shifted back in my sleep.

Someone brought me here.

That's when I feel it—heat, low and steady, beside me.

I turn my head.

Alexander.

He is lying beside me, one arm bent behind his head, eyes already on me like he hadn't slept at all. Like he'd spent the entire night watching me breathe.

His voice is soft, careful. "Should I go?"

I stare at him. The question sits between us like a blade.

And then something in me cracks.

"No," I say, and my voice came out hoarse. Raw.

I roll toward him, dragging the sheet with me. "No. I'm so sick of thinking. Of spiraling. Of drowning in all the questions I can't answer." My throat tightens. "I don't want to be inside my head anymore. I don't want to carry the prophecy or the bloodline or the weight of who I used to be."

His eyes darken.

I lean closer, breath brushing his jaw. "I want you to fuck me until I can't think. Until the world is just touch and skin and breath and *you*."

He doesn't move. Doesn't speak.

I press my lips to the corner of his mouth, soft and aching. "I want you to make me *feel,* Alexander. Nothing else. Just that. And then—" I swallow, heart racing. "When I'm right at the edge, when I can't take any more… I want you to bite me."

That does it.

His restraint shatters.

He pulls me from the bed, arms tight around my waist, mouth pressing to my neck like he couldn't decide whether to kiss me or devour me.

He leads me to the bathroom—slowly, deliberately—like he doesn't trust himself to move too fast.

"You're shaking," he murmurs, his knuckles grazing the sensitive skin at the inside of my thigh. I nod, barely breathing. "I can't help it, not when you touch me like that."

The shower steams around us as he undresses me piece by piece, fingertips brushing across my skin like silk. Like reverence.

He steps behind me in the water, letting the heat soak through us. His hands run over my shoulders, my back, my hips—soapy, slow, sliding over every curve like he is memorizing me by feel.

"You want to feel?" he says low, breath at my ear. "Then feel this."

His hands grip my waist as he pulls me back against him, the hard length of him pressing against my lower back. I arch instinctively, water trailing down my stomach as his mouth grazes the side of my neck.

He turns me, mouth finally claiming mine, slow and hot and consuming. His hand tangles in my hair. The other cups the back of my thigh and lifted, hoisting me effortlessly against the tile, water streaming over both of us.

He lines himself up, eyes locked on mine—hungry, reverent, wrecked. "Look at me," he breathes, voice rough silk. "I want to feel every inch of you fall apart around me."

He sinks in slowly—inch by inch—like he has all the time in the world and wants to savor the ruin. My breath hitches. My nails dig into his back. He doesn't stop.

"That's it," he whispers against my throat. "Take me in, sweetheart. Let me have all of you. No more running. No more hiding."

When he bottoms out, his mouth finds mine in a kiss that trembles between worship and need.

Every thrust is a question answered. Every kiss a vow unspoken.

His mouth moves lower. His hands worship. My body burns. And when I cry out, when the pressure in my core begins to spiral, he growled against my throat, low and possessive, like the sound was meant to brand me from the inside out. His hips press flush to mine, his body coils with tension, holding back the storm he's been threatening all night.

"Look at me, Jane. If I'm going to lose myself tonight, it will be deep inside you—every part of me that's craved you across lifetimes. Scream my name so they know you're mine, because no one will ever touch you the way I do, or claim you the way I already have."

The moan slips out before I can stop it, low and raw, as the heat coils tighter inside me—spiraling higher, sharp and sweet, until it threatens to break me open.

"Now?" he asks, voice shredded and dark with promise, his breath hot against my skin.

I barely manage a nod, my lips brushing his ear as I whisper, "Now."

He doesn't need more than that.

Just as the heat inside me shatters—sharp, blinding, deliciously unbearable—his fangs broke through skin and magic like silk tearing in candlelight.

The bite is everything.

Possession and prayer. Hunger and worship. It doesn't hurt—it claims.

A moan escapes me, broken and raw, as fire races from my throat to the base of my spine. My body arches into him, desperate for more, even as everything inside me surrenders completely.

He drinks like he's waited lifetimes for this. And maybe he has.

Pleasure and pain collide in a single, incandescent wave. I arch, legs tightening around his waist, the world going white at the edges.

There are no thoughts. Only feeling. Only him.

Afterward, Alexander holds me under the water, my back pressed to his chest, his arms around my waist like he could anchor me to this plane if he holds tight enough.

I let myself melt into him.

No prophecy. No wolf. No magic.

Just breath and steam and skin.

He wraps me in a towel and carried me back to bed, the scent of his skin mixing with the faint metallic tang of blood and something sweeter beneath it—something that makes me feel claimed. Desired.

He lays me down like I am something sacred, something breakable, then curls around me like he knew I wasn't.

His fingers trace the curve of my hip as he whispers something in a language I don't understand, his lips ghosting against my shoulder.

And for once, I don't ask.

I let the world fade.

I slip under, lulled by the warmth of his skin and the steady rhythm of his breath at my back.

Then—

The bar lights are low again. The music gone.

Only Maurice and I, breathless and electric in the back room—somewhere private and dim. The door clicks shut behind us, and he doesn't say a word as he walks me backward until my thighs bump the edge of the bar.

He lifts me like I weigh nothing, setting me onto the surface with that same look in his eyes I'd seen last night—hungry, focused. Possessive in a way that makes my knees weak and my pulse riot.

His hands skim up my thighs, slow and teasing, slipping just beneath the hem of my skirt.

I can feel him hard and insistent beneath his jeans, heat radiating between us.

"You remember what I said last night?" he asks, voice like smoke.

I swallow. "That I looked good enough to eat?"

He smirks, lowering to his knees. "Mmm. And baby…"

His hands part me, fingers gentle but sure.

"…I'm starving."

Then his mouth is on me—hot, deliberate, consuming.

I gasp, my back arching. The sensation is too sharp, too visceral to be a dream—

And that's when I feel it.

A mouth between my legs. Tongue. Hands. Heat. Real.

My body trembles, hips rolling forward on instinct, and I let my eyes flutter open—

Still half-lost in the haze of sleep.

But what I see made my heart stutter.

A man between my thighs.

For one fractured moment—brown eyes.

Maurice.

But then he looks up.

Not Maurice.

Alexander.

His lips are rosy. Eyes dark and half-lidded. His voice reverent, low, utterly wrecked.

"My God, baby," he breathes, tongue flicking against me again. "You're so wet."

My whole body jolts.

"Wait—" I choke, reaching down to still him with a trembling hand, mind scrambling to catch up with the blur of dream and reality.

He freezes immediately, lifting his head.

His brows furrow, not in frustration but concern. "Jane?"

I sit up fast, dragging the sheet with me. My chest heaves, but it isn't from arousal anymore.

"I—" I swallow hard. "I just… need a minute. I think I need some air."

Alexander's gaze sharpens, that ancient awareness flickering behind his eyes. He is too old, too experienced, not to notice the shift in me. His jaw tightens slightly.

"You okay?" he asks again, more slowly this time.

I nod too quickly. "Yeah. Just overstimulated. A little dizzy."

He doesn't call me on it.

Doesn't stop me.

But the way he watches me as I slide out of bed—gathering his over-sized shirt and tugging it on—told me he didn't buy a word.

Still, he gives me the grace of silence.

The stairs creak beneath me as I pad down into the dim light of the shop.

Séance & Sundry is still, wrapped in the hush of morning. The jars and shelves, the worn velvet chairs, and vintage register are all waiting in silence, like the shop knew I'm not ready to speak yet either.

No sign of Gran.

No incense burning. No kettle on.

Just the faint echo of my heartbeat and the cool wood under my feet.

I round the counter, needing something to do, maybe wipe down the glass or fix the crooked stack of herb bundles.

I can finally breathe, but the confusion clings anyway. Dreaming of Maurice, only to wake to Alexander—it's like my heart doesn't know which way to turn. One feels like a memory I've never lived, the other like a future I'm too afraid to want. And somewhere in between, I'm left wondering if either choice is really mine.

Then I see it—a note, half-tucked beneath the front door.

I crouch and pull it free.

The paper is worn, damp at the edges from morning dew. My name is written in unfamiliar ink.

Inside: Meet me in the bayou. Alone. Where you shifted. Tell no one.

No signature. No threat. Just direction—and a chill that skates down my spine.

Every instinct says not to go.

But I already know I will.

Because whatever's waiting for me there isn't just about me anymore. It never was.

I shove the note in my pocket, grab my boots, and step into the rising heat of the day.

Meet me in the bayou. Alone. Where you shifted. Tell no one.

I stared at the note, the air suddenly too thick to breathe. My mind was buzzing with everything I didn't want to think about—Alexander upstairs, warm and waiting. The dream is still echoing behind my eyes. Maurice's mouth, his voice—

I pressed my palm against the counter and exhaled slowly.

I didn't want to leave him.

But I had to.

CHAPTER SIXTEEN

BLOODLINES AND BAYOUS

The words burn through me on repeat as I walk— *Meet me in the bayou. Alone. Where you shifted. Tell no one.*

Each step down the winding path feels heavier than the last, like the trees are pulling at my limbs, warning me not to go. My boots sink into the moss with wet squelches. Branches snap in the distance, too deliberate to be random. The cicadas scream like prophets overhead, shrill and relentless.

I smell smoke.

No—ash. Not fresh. Something old. Lingering.

A memory. A warning.

My breath hitches as I step into the clearing.

It still hums. Still holds the echo of the blood moon, of the shift that tore me open and rebuilt me.

And someone is watching.

I feel it in the back of my neck, the weight of unseen eyes, of breath held just beyond the tree line.

Then he steps out.

Samuel Delacroix.

He emerges like he's been waiting there for hours, arms loose at his sides, coat unbuttoned. He looks calm. But I see the flicker in his eyes. The stiffness in his shoulders. He is braced.

Waiting for the storm.

"I didn't mean to kill her," he says without preamble. "Only him. Your father."

The words strike like a rock through glass. My body locks tight. But I don't speak.

"She wasn't supposed to be part of it. She got in the way," he goes on, voice low. "Jumped between us. The bite—was an accident. I didn't mean for it to land on her. But it did. And it killed her."

My breath turns to stone in my lungs.

"She died trying to protect him," he adds quietly. "And I live with that."

His face twists for the first time—just slightly. Like saying it out loud cracks something in him too.

He looks away. Into the trees. Or into the past.

"He was having an affair," he says. "With my wife."

My stomach turns.

"Braelynn's mother," he clarifies. "She was vulnerable. And he was charming. Too charming. The kind of man who could make you forget your own name, let alone your vows."

He exhales through his nose. "I think he took advantage of that. Though she denied it saying it was a mistake amongst friends going through hard times."

There is no anger in his voice when he says her name. Only a weariness. The sound of a man who'd ruined something and didn't know how to rebuild it.

"She got pregnant," he says, glancing back at me now. "And I didn't know how to carry it. I'd never heard of a wolf and a witch conceiving. It shouldn't have been possible."

His eyes search mine like he was still looking for logic. "Wolf venom doesn't turn witches. It kills them. You're born a wolf, or you're not. So thought the baby had to be mine then."

His voice drops even lower.

"But then I saw you shift. Under the blood moon. Saw the way your fur matched hers. And I knew. You and Braelynn weren't just linked by blood. You share something unnatural. Something that shouldn't be."

My fingers twitch.

Heat surges beneath my skin like rising smoke, licking at the back of my neck.

And still, he speaks.

"I realized what he passed on. Your father. What he left behind when he touched something sacred that didn't belong to him."

My jaw locks. My teeth ache from clenching.

My thoughts come in flames: I want to burn his words before they touch me. But they're already in my bones. Already searing holes through everything I thought I knew.

I take one step closer.

"You killed my parents," I say, voice trembling but sharp. "For pride. For betrayal. For pain you didn't know what to do with. And now you want to tell me you regret it like that's supposed to mean something?"

The air around me shifts—subtle but wrong.

Magic is rising. Crawling up my spine. Coiling behind my ribs like it had teeth.

"You don't know what you've done," I say, breath hitching. "You don't know who you've crossed."

I lift my chin slowly to look at him.

Samuel's expression falters just for a second.

And then his eyes widen slightly. "Your eyes," he murmurs. "They've changed."

I don't blink. Don't breathe.

My fingers spark—tiny flickers of blue light snapping between them like impatient fireflies. My hair lifts slightly, caught in a wind only I could feel.

And behind me—footsteps.

"Jane—?" Braelynn's voice cracks at the edge of the clearing.

I don't turn. I feel her. Her grief. Her fear.

And Maurice beside her—solid, steady. Always just close enough to catch me.

But not this time.

This time, I don't need to be caught.

I need to burn.

"Run," I say, voice low but thick with power. "RUN…before I do something I might someday regret!"

He doesn't wait.

He turns and flees, crashing into the woods like a man being chased by something not quite human.

He isn't wrong.

The second he disappears, the storm breaks.

A scream tears from my throat—so raw it barely sounds like a voice at all. It is magic. Unfiltered. Pure.

And the earth answers.

The moss beneath me hisses, then catches—flames spiraling outward in a perfect ring. Orange and gold and white-hot, fed by no fuel, needing no air.

My hands are shaking violently. Sparks leap from my fingertips and lick up my arms.

Lightning bleeds into the sky, veins of white and blue tearing across the clouds until one strikes the clearing directly—a bolt so loud it shatters the silence, splitting a nearby tree from root to crown.

The air bends. Sound cracks. The bayou ignites.

Wind whips around me in a cyclone of ash and power, my hair lashing like a banner behind me. I feel the heat inside me expanding, stretching, wanting.

I drop to my knees, and the ground doesn't just shake—it shudders.

The fire swirls around me like it is dancing. Like it knows me.

And through it all, I feel the ground press back. Feel the world inhale. And still—I'm not done.

Braelynn is beside me in seconds, her knees hitting the moss, tears streaking down her cheeks as her hand lands on my shoulder.

Maurice follows, crouching, arms around us both, jaw clenched as he holds us steady.

We don't speak.

We don't need to.

Only the storm speaks now. Only the fire. Only the wild, unrelenting magic that finally stopped hiding and the truth B and I now have to face, as sisters.

CHAPTER SEVENTEEN

THE WEIGHT OF WHAT REMAINS

E veryone parts ways after the bayou.

No dramatic exits. No goodbyes. Just quiet.

Even that feels like too much.

Back at the shop, later that evening, Gran keeps her tone steady, but I can feel the tremble beneath her words when she tells me: "He's on the run, Janey. But he won't get far."

She sits me down, brushing my hair out of my face like I'm still small, still hers. "Samuel broke the oath pact between the coven and the pack. He took two witches from this world—one intentionally, one through chaos. That breach demands justice. You know what that means."

I nod, hollow. "Execution."

Her hand squeezes mine. "He'll be tracked. The Council will make sure of it."

I want to feel relief. But I just feel tired as Gran heads upstairs to her apartment.

The sun's barely dipped behind the Quarter when there's a knock at the back door of the shop as I close up.

Maurice.

His frame fills the doorway like a question he's not sure he should ask. But I let him in.

He doesn't sit. Just paces once. Then twice. Then—

"I know this isn't fair timing," he says, voice rough. "I know you've got about ten thousand bigger things on your mind right now, and I sure as hell didn't plan to do this like some lovesick teenager."

He stops.

"But I need to say it."

I wait.

"I think I started loving you before I even knew what love was. Before I knew what it meant to ache just from the sound of someone's laughter fading as they walked away.

"You were always a gravity I didn't understand—pulling me in, even when I told myself I had no right to want more than friendship. I convinced myself I could live at the edge of your orbit. Close enough to feel your warmth. Far enough not to burn.

"But I lied. To you. To myself.

"Jane, loving you has never been quiet for me. It's thunder under my ribs. It's every word I never said, carved into bone. It's watching you choose everyone but me, and still praying you find happiness, even if I'm not the one holding your hand when it comes.

"You are my before and my after. You are every calm I chased and every storm I'd Walk into without hesitation.

"If fate had written a different story, I'd still choose you—even if it meant I'd only get to watch you love someone else. But gods help me… if there's even a fragment of you that's mine, I'll spend whatever life I have left proving I was always yours.

"I love you, Jane," he says. "Long before this mating bond bullshit. Before you shifted. Before the prophecy. Before I knew what any of this meant."

My breath catches, but he presses on.

"That vampire—Alexander—he might've had you in another life, but he can't give you what you want in this one. Not really. He's dead. That's what vampires are. Dead things that walk. They don't grow. They

don't age. They don't change. You think he can give you a family? A future? The kind of life you deserve?"

I flinch, but he softens. Moves closer.

"I know you feel something for him. Hell, I'd be blind not to see it. But Jane…" He reaches out, fingertips brushing mine. "You could have something real. Here. With me. I'm not asking for anything right now—not when your whole world's coming apart—but I had to tell you. Before you make any decision that locks you into something you can't come back from."

His lips press against mine. Gentle. Reverent. A whisper of a kiss meant for goodbye…or maybe something more. My heart is thunderous, and I hear the weather shift outside as a storm rolls in. Fitting.

Then he leaves.

No demand. No lingering look. Just the sound of his boots on the wood, the soft click of the back door, and silence.

I climb the stairs to my room, each step heavier than the last.

I don't expect him.

But he's there.

Alexander stands by the window, moonlight tracing his silhouette like a ghost from a better story. The rain hits the balcony in a steady rhythm. He doesn't speak. Just looks at me, blue eyes stormy but calm.

"I heard everything," he says quietly. "Vampire hearing. It's a curse sometimes."

I cross to him slowly. He meets me in the middle.

He lifts a hand and brushes a strand of hair behind my ear.

Then leans in. A kiss, soft as dusk, lands on my forehead.

"Do you want me to stay?"

His voice doesn't crack. Mine almost does.

I shake my head no. My eyes fill with tears, but I don't let them fall.

He nods once.

And then he's gone. Out the balcony window like a wisp of fog— here, then not.

The house is quiet.

Gran's gone to bed. The shop is closed. Even the air feels still, like the whole world is holding its breath.

I sit alone on the edge of my bed, too restless to sleep, too raw to cry.

Then I feel it.

A pulse. Gentle. Persistent. Like a heartbeat beneath the floorboards.

I drop to my knees, reach beneath the bed, and slide out the grimoire.

The leather is warm beneath my fingers. Warmer than it should be. The sigil on the front, once dormant, now glows faintly with silver light, crackling like distant thunder.

It's unlocked.

The grimoire opens on its own.

Pages flutter in a blur, whipped by a wind that isn't there, stopping only when the right one finds me.

Symbols shift. Rearranging. Translating.

Ink rises and melts and reforms—cold magic crawling across the parchment like frost under moonlight.

And then it speaks.

The Velashara Prophecy

Born of soul and blood made one, From storm's breath and shadowed sun. Where truths divide and silence clings, A child shall rise with shattered wings.

Of lightning's line and dragon's flame, A soul returns, but not the same. When blood moon bleeds and veil is thin, Old hunger wakes from deep within.

From witch's womb and venom's bite, A hybrid stirs beneath the night. Two lines, unmixed, now fate has crossed—A reckoning found, a balance lost.

In one, the bloodline sealed and true. In one, the soul the fire knew.

The gate once opened must be closed, Lest Eternal thirst be reimposed.

But soul keepers, bound by vow and breath, Alone may seal the wound of death.

The fire of the dragon—white as snow, Marked in black where shadows grow. The lightning in the witch's vein, Together strike to break the chain.

Yet power given is not the key—The cost is life. The bond set free. One must fall so one may live. A soul to take. A soul to give.

The Velashara line shall burn anew, Through ash and bloom, through dusk and dew. But beware the kiss that feels like grace—For love may shift the final face.

The pages go still. The glow fades. I sit frozen, the chill of the spell still wrapped around me like a shroud. I don't understand all of it. Not yet. But I understand enough.

Lightning and fire. Witch and dragon. Me and Alexander.

We're both soul keepers.

Two halves of something ancient. A lock and a key. A fire and a fuse. But what does it really mean?

The prophecy speaks in riddles and sacrifice. Of doors that must be closed and prices that must be paid. It speaks of life and death and love twisted into something bigger than both of us. And I don't know yet where I fit inside all of it.

Or what I'll be asked to give up.

It's too much to unpack tonight. My mind feels like it's splintering at the edges, too full, too bright, too loud. Like my body hasn't caught up with what my soul already knows. I can still feel the echo of my shift humming in my bones, still feel the electric charge of Maurice's words, the weight of Alexander's goodbye, the unspoken terror in Gran's touch.

My parents. Their deaths weren't just a tragedy. They were a turning point. A ripple set loose across time. And now I know the truth—some of it, anyway. But I get the sense there's more waiting. Beneath the surface. Beneath the stone. Behind the veil of what I've just begun to understand.

The grimoire said the gate must be closed. That only soul keepers can do it. But it didn't say how. It didn't say when. And it didn't say what happens if we fail.

All I know is that something is coming.

The blood moon was only the beginning. A warning shot. A turning tide. Whatever comes next—whatever test this prophecy intends to deliver—it's no longer about just me.

It's about the bond between soul and blood. The magic that made me. The love that might destroy me. And the enemies watching from the shadows, waiting for me to stumble.

I close the grimoire, the echo of its magic still cold against my fingertips.

Tomorrow, I'll face the storm. Tonight, I just try to breathe and rest.

That night, I dream. But it doesn't feel like a dream.

I stand at the edge of something ancient. Cold stone. Flickering torchlight. Shadows twisted in cloaks and silence.

A meeting. A council.

The rogue vampires have gathered in a half-circle around a fireless brazier, their whispers like broken promises, their eyes hungry with unrest.

Someone steps forward from the shadows, whispering with suspicion.

"Morgaine," one of the vampires says.

She steps forward with a vampire flanking her side.

The name flickers across my mind like static and then settles with a cold, sharp certainty.

I've heard it before.

From Alexander.

He mentioned her about five years ago. A seer. A powerful one. Not aligned with any coven, but somehow always right. He said she kept to herself, walked between the lines. That she helped him avoid danger when rogue vampires began rising again. That she'd earned his trust.

He never said she was involved with the rogue faction.

Never said she was tied to anything this dark.

Never said she was working both sides.

But now, I see her clearly.

She stands among the rogues, robed in midnight, her eyes glowing with layered magic. Not just red. Not just gold. Something older. Something dangerous.

A witch…and more than a witch. A traitor in silk.

My chest tightens. Alexander doesn't know.

He thinks she's still helping. Still watching the horizon for threats, not conjuring them behind his back. He doesn't see the way her presence at that circle feels like a blessing, like a signal that whatever is coming has already begun.

And me? I've been playing right into it. Trust no one—that's what Gran always said. But I trusted him. And he trusted her.

Now I see how far this betrayal stretches.

Not just the betrayal of the Velashara line, but of Alexander too.

And the vampire next to her, I recognize him. I passed him on my way to Jackson Square the night of our book club meeting. He locked eyes with me, longer than what was considered polite, with the bright blonde hair. Then he disappeared.

"Morgaine," one of the cloaked vampires murmurs again, stepping forward. "What have you seen?"

She lifts her chin, eyes bright with knowing.

"I saw her," she says, calm and absolute. "She is no longer hidden."

A low wave of whispers rolls through the council like a tide. Shifting cloaks. Gleaming teeth. Hunger, barely leashed.

Morgaine smiles faintly, like she's kept secret just long enough.

Then, softly—almost reverently—she says:

"The Velashara Line lives."

I wake with a jolt, the last words still echoing in my head.

And I know the hunt has already begun.

CHARACTER GLOSSARY

Jane Agatha Fontenot

Age: 29

Role: Protagonist, witch from New Orleans.

Description: Curvy frame, green eyes, brunette hair. Neurodivergent, introspective, deeply empathetic.

Personality: Quiet strength, sharp wit, loyal, often caught between self-doubt and resilience.

Profile: Raised by her grandmother after the loss of her parents, Jane has always felt the spark of something more beneath the surface of her life. Approaching her thirtieth birthday, she finds herself drawn into mysteries and powers she never expected.

Scent Profile: Warm vanilla and rain-kissed stone, threaded with a spark of ozone.

Agatha Velashara Fontenot (Gran)

Age: 73

Role: Jane's grandmother, witch, leader of the New Orleans coven.

Description: Silver-gray hair, green eyes, flowing skirts and rings. Moves with quiet strength.

Personality: Wise, loving, fiercely protective, bearer of secrets.

Profile: As the matriarch of her family, Agatha raised Jane after tragedy. She once served on the witch council but stepped back to run Séance & Sundry and mentor young witches more directly. Her choice to lead the New Orleans coven hands-on keeps her close to her granddaughter while still guiding her community.

Scent Profile: Dried sage, beeswax candles, and herbal tea.

Alexander

Age: Appears 30s (immortal vampire)

Role: Vampire, enigmatic soul keeper.

Description: Sandy-blond hair, dark blue eyes, alluring and dangerous presence.

Personality: Seductive, protective, conflicted, centuries of longing beneath his charm.

Profile: Once bound to Jane's soul in another lifetime, Alexander's return stirs passions and dangers that test the boundaries of memory, magic, and fate.

Scent Profile: Smoked cedar, old leather, and the faintest trace of wine-dark roses.

Maurice Delacroix

Age: 32

Role: Wolf shifter, Jane's lifelong friend.

Description: Tall, warm brown skin, kind eyes, steady strength.

Personality: Patient, dependable, protective, quiet passion beneath calm.

Profile: A childhood friend of Jane's, Maurice blends the heart of a teacher with the instincts of a wolf. His loyalty and constancy make him a grounding presence in her life.

Scent Profile: Fresh cedarwood, sun-warmed cotton, and the sweetness of amber.

Braelynn "B" Delacroix

Age: 29

Role: Jane's best friend, wolf shifter.

Description: Mixed heritage, striking presence, rare white wolf form with a black streak.

Personality: Bold, outspoken, fiercely loyal, playful yet protective.

Profile: Braelynn has always stood at Jane's side, unafraid to challenge expectations. Her unique wolf form marks her as rare within the pack, and her fire makes her unforgettable.

Scent Profile: Wild jasmine and citrus peel with an undercurrent of smoke.

Javi De la Rosa

Age: 27

Role: Witch, performer, chosen family.

Description: Olive-toned skin, bold style, expressive eyes.

Personality: Spicy, sassy, glittering confidence with a tender heart.

Profile: Fierce and fabulous, Javi protects his chosen family with both fire and softness. He carries the rare gift of making others laugh while reminding them of their worth.

Scent Profile: Cinnamon, cloves, and sweet vanilla cream.

Fergus

Age: 30

Role: Wolf shifter, protector, chosen family.

Description: Tall, lean muscle, steady eyes, watchful presence.

Personality: Quiet, grounded, observant, gentle strength.

Profile: Fergus is the steady backbone of his circle—rarely loud, but always present. His loyalty and quiet wisdom make him someone others lean on without even realizing it.

Scent Profile: Pine needles, clean musk, and cool river stone.

Kaia Ruelle

Age: 28

Role: Wolf shifter, Braelynn's close companion.

Description: Olive skin, chestnut eyes, ice-blond bob with black roots, glyph tattoos.

Personality: Edgy, confident, protective, fiercely independent.

Profile: A survivor of a splinter pack, Kaia forged her own path as a tattoo artist and fighter. Her presence evokes both danger and devotion.

Scent Profile: Ink, leather, and wild mint.

Samuel Delacroix

Age: 50s

Role: Packmaster of the New Orleans wolves.

Description: Stern presence, commanding wolf shifter.

Personality: Authoritative, disciplined, protective of his pack.

Profile: As Packmaster, Samuel bears the burden of leadership, striving to maintain balance between wolves and the other supernatural communities of New Orleans.

Scent Profile: Tobacco, oak, and iron-tinged earth.

About the Author

Jaclyn Bales has been writing since child-hood, when she first discovered the magic of creating entire worlds beneath the branches of a maple tree. For her, writing has always been both a form of healing and a kind of spell—words carrying ache, wonder, and hope in equal measure.

She pursued her passion academically, completing advanced English and creative literature courses in college, where she honed her craft and developed her distinctive voice. With a lifelong love of Southern Gothic atmosphere, romantic fantasy, and the power of found family, she uses her work to blend emotional depth with imaginative storytelling.

Her debut novella, Plain Jane: The Awakening—Book One of the Soul Lineage Trilogy—introduces readers to a hauntingly magical New Orleans where witches, wolves, vampires, and dragon-blooded legacies collide.

Jaclyn is continually inspired by the belief that even in the darkest chapters, the moon remembers our name.

WHEN FATE CALLS, BLOOD LISTENS.

Jane Agatha Fontenot has never felt like she belonged.
Not with her curvy frame, her neurodivergent mind,
or the flickers of magic that sparked and faded without reason.
To her grandmother she's still "Janey."
To her best friend, simply "J."
But to world at large? Fogettable. Ordinary

THEY COULDN'T BE MORE WRONG.

Born beneath a blood moon that claimed her mothers life,
Jane carries the reincarnated soul of a witch burned centuries ago.
Paired with her hidden bloodline, that soul holds a magic unseen
for generations.
And now, as her thirtieth birthday approaches,
on the first blood moon since her birth,
the dormant power stirs awake...

ALONG WITH IT COMES THE MEMORIES...
THE MAGIC...
AND HIM.

Lurking just beyond the veil of the ordinary world is the man her soul has
loved across lifetimes, finally drawn back to her after centuries apart.
But not everyone welcomes her return. As old enemies stir and
long-buried secrets rise, Jane must embrace who she was to survive who
she is becoming.

SHE THOUGHT SHE WAS PLAIN.
SHE WAS NEVER PLAIN.
SHE WAS CHOSEN.

ISBN 979-8-218-79341-8
9 798218 793418

A FORBIDDEN ROMANCE
BROKEN
BEAUTIFUL
LIES
MARY JAAY